CHERISH AND PROTECT

BOOK SIX IN THE HEROES OF EVERS, TX SERIES

LORI RYAN

OTHER BOOKS BY LORI RYAN

Promise and Protect

Honor and Protect (An Evers, TX Novella)

Serve and Protect

Desire and Protect

Cherish and Protect

Treasure and Protect

The Dark Falls, CO Series:

Dark Falls

Dark Burning

Dark Prison

Coming Soon – The Halo Security Series:

Dulce's Defender

Hannah's Hero

Shay's Shelter

Callie's Cover

Grace's Guardian

Sophie's Sentry

Sienna's Sentinal

For the most current list of Lori's books, visit her website: loriryanromance.com.

CHAPTER ONE

He probably shouldn't have been so comfortable in the dark.

In fact, most would guess he'd crave the sun and want to sleep out in the open after what he'd been through, but that wasn't the way things had worked out. He'd spent nearly five years as a prisoner of dark rooms where he'd been starved and left to rot, but James Keegan Lawless somehow seemed to need the dark.

The barn his sister and her family had converted to an apartment for him served those needs most days, so long as he didn't throw open the doors and turn on all the lights. He lived in the converted loft, but the lower half was still one large workspace. Laura had said it once belonged to her husband's father, a man who liked inventing things more than working the ranch.

James wasn't working with the saw today, so he only flicked on the lights near the workbench, leaving the rest of the space gray.

"Go lay down, Lu," James said in a voice so low only the dog he spoke to would hear it. Lulu, the large Pyrenees mix his brother-in-law had trained as a service dog for him, seemed to always have her ears trained toward him, making anything louder unnecessary. Thankfully.

He hadn't expected the dog to help much when he came to the ranch two months back, but he had to admit, she was growing on him. Talking to her was easier than talking to anyone else.

Not that he talked to her about anything deep or important. He rarely said more than a few words at a time. She didn't seem to mind.

Just opening his mouth and saying anything nowadays was hard. Then again, he'd never been big on words. Still, somehow, in the jungles of South America, in a small area called the Devil's Den by those who spent any time there, the words seemed to have been stripped from him. Words, humanity, his soul.

The dog didn't judge. She padded over to the blanket he'd tossed on the ground in the corner for her and tucked her paws under her chin. Sentry. She stood sentry over him.

James went to the corner and lifted the sandpaper he'd left there the night before, folding it several times to get a clean spot before applying it to the wooden shelf he was making. He should do a table and chairs next. The loft had a small set, of course, but the one down here in the workroom was old. He could do better.

Lulu's head came up and James nodded. "Yeah, I hear her too."

The dog looked at him as if to say, "What do you plan to do about it?"

"Not a damned thing," he answered as he pictured the woman out there, strong and sure as the devil herself on top of that horse. He knew she'd do a few laps of the ring to warm her horse up, then she'd send the horse over jumps so tall and wide they could make your heart hold its breath, as she and the powerful beast strode toward them.

She would laugh when she landed, and he didn't blame her. She was flying, after all.

According to Laura, the jumps the woman was taking weren't even as high as they could be. The horse she kept here at Bishop Ranch was a retired Grand Prix jumper, so she only took her over five-foot jumps, not anything higher.

James moved his hands over the wood. Solid, smooth, steady under his hands.

Lulu stood and moved on quiet feet to the door, looking out through the crack where the edge of it almost met the side wall. She breathed in a deep gulp of air and he wondered at all she might take in with that breath. He'd heard that when a dog was sniffing, it was like it was reading the newspaper. They pulled volumes of information in through those sensitized noses of theirs.

James froze for a split second as his thoughts went involuntarily to what *she* would smell like. The goddess on the horse. That's how he thought of her. Not because she was gorgeous, though she was. No, she was a goddess because of her strength. She rode on that beast like it was nothing, took those jumps as if they were two inches tall instead of five feet.

So, yeah, she was a goddess.

"Lu, bed." He pointed to the blanket and the dog went, looking at him like he'd stolen a donut right out from under her nose.

"I don't know why you're so fascinated with her anyway," he said, to himself and the dog.

He started the careful job of applying glue, then fitting together the last of the dovetail joints that would secure the top of the bookcase to the body. He wondered idly how many pieces of furniture he could make before he ran out of space to store them. Maybe Laura and Cade could take some to their house.

Then again, he thought with a glance around, if he stacked them to the ceiling, he could fit a lot in the barn.

Lu's head came up again and Cade heard the footsteps that had spurred the movement. Not human footsteps. A horse.

James tossed his rag on the table and issued a low whistle to the dog before retreating up the stairs to the loft.

Could be it was Cade coming to see him.

Or not. Better to watch from his stairs so he could escape up to the loft if he needed to.

PRESLEY ROYALE SLOWED as she neared the barn. She wouldn't knock or say hello. She never did. She knew Laura's brother, James, lived there and from what she could gather, he didn't want visitors. She could respect that. If anyone could understand that not everyone wanted to see or talk to people, it was Presley.

Much to her parents' dismay, she wasn't born wanting to be the center of attention. She would rather go home and bed the horses down for the night, then read a book in bed. They wanted to drag her to whatever wine and cheese or victory party was taking place after the show.

Still, she liked circling out near the old barn to cool down Tess after a ride. The view behind the barn was gorgeous for a lot of reasons. In the spring, there were wild flowers dotting the landscape in slashes of bright color. But even now, in the dry summer, there was a beauty to the yellow grass that blew in the breeze. She wondered what it would look like in the fall. There were a few trees out on the horizon, and even though fall in Texas had nothing on the changing leaves of New England, they would turn orange or yellow. Presley would bet it was pretty.

She murmured to Tess and made the almost unconscious gestures that would move the horse around to loop the older barn before walking back to the newer barn that now housed the animals. She'd have to ask Laura if they had names for the different barns. Although, she guessed now this one should really be called James's barn regardless of what it had been called before.

Presley was too deep in thought for her own good when Tess startled and shied, catching Presley off guard. She gripped with her legs and dug her hands into the mane. Presley would figure out what had spooked the horse later. For now, she needed to keep her mount.

As with anything having to do with horses, fractions of a second changed the situation. It quickly became clear that keeping her mount was the last thing Presley needed to do as Tess stumbled sideways and fell. Presley threw herself, trying to clear the space before a thousand pounds of lean muscular horse flesh came down on her, pinning her to the ground or breaking a leg.

She almost made it.

Presley looked up from her string of curses in time to see that someone had witnessed her creative burst of frustration.

She didn't have much time to process the man standing over her as he steadied Tess by the reins, before cursing again as Tess grunted and tried to right herself.

"Stop her!" Presley held out a hand to the man. "Hold

her reins and try not to let her move. I don't want her to hurt herself."

He shot her a look, but held the reins firm while Presley half dragged, half limped, but mostly scrambled to Tess's head. She *shooshed* and steadied the mare for several seconds, making sure she was calm. If Tess tried to get up while she was still panicked, she was more likely to injure herself in the process. Presley pushed herself to a standing position, leaning most of her weight on her one good foot.

A few clucks of her tongue and Tess was on her feet. Presley eyed the horse from where she stood. She needed to feel her legs, check them for injuries. The only problem was, when Tess had gone down, she'd fallen on Presley's left foot and she was guessing from the amount of pain she was in, she had likely suffered a bad sprain. She didn't think it could be a break, but she also wasn't eager to find out by trying to walk on it and failing.

"Do you know anything about horses?" She asked. She could feel him behind her. He was that kind of man, the one you felt straight on through to your toes. She kept her voice steady and soothing with the question, still rubbing one hand up and down the flat of Tess's face.

"Some." It occurred to Presley that the man hadn't said a word until then, and she wondered if he only spoke in one-word sentences. Though, she supposed, a single word couldn't really be called a sentence.

"Enough to run your hands down her legs without getting yourself kicked?"

He didn't answer. Just moved silently to her left and began to do as she'd asked. He seemed to know what he was doing, taking up a position that kept his back to Presley as he faced the horse's rear and bent to run his hand gently down the front right leg.

"They won't be swollen or warm yet, so just look for cuts," she said.

He nodded and moved to the back leg next and so on. It was a position that allowed her to see his jean-clad ass in a way that shouldn't have been so distracting given her level of concern for Tess.

He stood and turned Presley's way.

"No cuts."

Two words this time.

Presley nodded. She would check for herself about twenty more times before she put Tess up for the day, but this would have to do for now.

"Thank you," she said looking at the ground. "We should figure out what spooked her. She doesn't shy easily, so there had to be a snake or something."

The man, who she assumed was Laura's brother James, pointed to a spot on the ground behind her. The body of a snake sat cut in half but still writhing some ten feet away.

"Oh." Presley couldn't really think of much more to say to that. She saw a shovel laying nearby and put two-and-two together. "That was fast."

She thought she saw James's lips twitch, but if they had, he halted the action before a smile could appear on his face.

A beautiful white dog sat in the door to the barn, alternately looking between the man and the snake.

"That's not for you, Lu," James said, only the slightest edge of warning tempering his tone.

"Will she listen? A snake head can bite for up to an hour after it's been cut off."

The dog answered for James, backing up a few feet before laying down, head on paws and watching them.

"Okay, then," Presley said. She hopped on her good foot to stand at Tess's side and took hold of her mane with one hand, preparing to limp it back to the animal barn so she could get Tess on crossties and check her legs herself. She needed to watch for heat or swelling, which would indicate there was inflammation from an injury.

That was how she'd started thinking of Tess's barn. There was the animal barn and the brother barn.

The thought made her picture a barn full of sexy, brooding brothers that had asses to die for and eyes that seemed to see into a person's soul. Not a bad way to use a barn.

Wow. Those were new thoughts for Presley.

"I don't think so," James said quietly and slid his arms around her waist, somehow taking the reins of her horse at the same time.

"Excuse me? I need to get Tess put up."

He snorted.

"What are you doing?" Presley asked as he moved her over to a large rock near a tree and settled her on it. He led Tess down to a small pasture that sat between the riding ring and the brother barn. Presley watched as he stripped the horse of saddle and bridle and let her into the pasture. The competency of his movements was the only thing that overcame her irritation at him. That, and the fact his actions had given her a chance to watch Tess as she walked beside him. Given Tess's steady gait, the horse probably wasn't injured.

Then James was back and crouched before her, raising a hand to the side of her head. She realized she still wore her helmet and raised her hands to take it off, but he pushed them aside.

"You're bleeding."

"I'm what?" She raised her hands one more, this time intending to feel for blood.

He grunted and moved them aside again, replacing them with his own. He held her head in place with his right hand and prodded softly on her temple with the left.

"I thought you couldn't fall," he murmured as he worked.

"What?"

He didn't answer.

"What would make you think I couldn't fall?" Presley didn't ask the other questions running through her head. *You know who I am? Enough to have thoughts about me? As in, you're thinking about me?*

He brushed along her left cheek with his thumb but remained silent.

Presley did not. "I don't fall often, I guess, but believe me, there are times you can't help it. For one thing, if your horse goes down, you're going to go down, too." When Tess had stumbled, there was really no way for Presley not to go with her. It was physics, and physics ruled a lot of what happened on a horse. "And if you have over a thousand pounds of muscle moving under you at top speed and it decides to stop with no warning..." she didn't finish the statement.

Truth was, she could usually keep her seat when Tess did that nowadays. She could often keep her seat on any horse, but there were always falls. Any rider who said they didn't fall was talking crap.

Mostly she was talking now just for the sake of talking. He didn't seem to want to fill the quiet and she suddenly needed to, which was a little out of character for her.

With a grunt, he stood. "It's just a scratch."

He turned and walked through the door to the barn, the dog turning and following him as he passed.

Presley sat on the rock, wondering if that was the end of

it. No hello. No goodbye. It had been the strangest encounter she'd ever, well, encountered.

She stood, looking over to where Tess stood lazily munching on grass. Presley blew out a breath of air, ready to attempt the hobble back to the animal barn. She took a limping step toward the pasture and flinched.

"Boy, you can't sit still, can you?"

She spun at the words, then toppled sideways and began that pinwheeling thing with her arms that people think can only happen in a cartoon. Until it happens. With a witness.

Then there were strong hands on her waist again. A little pressure from those hands and she was sinking back down onto the rock again. He produced a first aid kit and pulled a bandage from it, putting it on her temple as she sat stone still.

His face was right next to hers as he doctored her, and Lord, but the man smelled good. Insanely good.

Then his hands were moving down her leg, and she sucked in a breath, making him still.

"Did I hurt you?" He asked, looking at her now.

She shook her head, probably a little too quickly, too emphatically.

He watched her face for a minute then turned his attention back to his ministrations, pulling her boot from her foot. The fleeting hope that her feet didn't smell flitted through her brain, a brain that was apparently becoming addled in his presence.

"I'm Presley," she said.

He continued to pull her sock down and examine the swelling in her ankle. It seemed to be blowing up at an alarming rate now that the boot had been removed. He pulled an instant ice pack from the first aid kit and cracked it to activate the cold. She'd always liked that moment of cracking the ice for some reason.

"You're James," she said, though her head was screaming she was an idiot for telling him who he was. His lips twitched but she didn't know if he was fighting off a smile or frown.

She winced as he wrapped her foot in an ACE bandage, stopping after a few rotations to place the ice pack against the center of the swelling, then using the bandage to hold it in place.

He stood and held out his hand. Slipping hers into it shouldn't have felt so good, but it did. His hand was warm, strong, and steady as he pulled her to her feet. She ignored it.

"Okay, well, it was nice to meet you, James." Clearly, there had been no actual *meeting* since that would require him introducing himself and going through the kind of introductory comments that typically went along with it. *Good to meet you, I've been looking forward to meeting you,* that sort of thing.

Presley suppressed a laugh at the thought that she was the talkative one in the conversation. Not at all something she'd been able to claim in the past.

He put a hand on her shoulder, holding her in place, while he pulled his phone from his pocket and hit a few keys.

"Hey Cade, it's James. Can you come over to the barn? Presley hurt her ankle. I don't think it's broken but she should have an X-ray in case there's a hairline fracture."

"That was a lot of words." She couldn't help it. It was the first thought that popped into her head.

"Yeah," he said, scrubbing at the back of his head with one hand and looking a little embarrassed.

Presley felt her cheeks heat. She hadn't meant to make him feel bad. "I'm sorry." She bit down on the urge to tell him she didn't always know the right thing to say, and often felt like she said the exact opposite most of the time. She weighed the chances he might think she was crazy for trying to explain herself against wanting him to realize she hadn't meant to be a bitch, but before she could make a decision, Cade and Laura came around the side of the barn.

And while a plan was made for Laura to drive Presley to the hospital despite her objections and for Cade to take Tess back to the barn to thoroughly check her out, James Lawless slipped back into the quiet blackness of the barn behind them.

CHAPTER TWO

Presley got out of the car and waited while Laura slid the crutches she'd rented from the hospital pharmacy out of the back seat.

"Thank you," Presley murmured as Laura handed her first one, then the other. She turned and looked at the stable where her father would be, then back up at the house where she knew her mother would be waiting.

She didn't know which one of them she preferred to face first. Since her leg was throbbing, she supposed going up to the house was her best bet. Her mother would likely call her father as soon as she saw the air cast on Presley's leg anyway, so she might as well be someplace she could sit and elevate her ankle.

"I'll help you into the house," Laura said.

Presley nodded. She'd like to say no, but the fact was, it would be a lot easier for her to get up the stairs if Laura was there to hold the crutches.

She could have had Laura take her around to the apartment she lived in at the back of the house, but really, she had to face her parents eventually and getting it over with was probably the best course of action.

They'd made it to the base of the steps leading to the wide stone porch when the door opened and her mother came out.

"Pres, what happened?"

Presley stopped and looked up to find a face that was nearly her mirror in every way, with dark brown hair and blue eyes. They might be sisters were it not for the plastic surgery that had seemed to stretch her mother's features over time. Still, the woman was beautiful. Just, a little preserved looking.

"I had an accident on Tess."

Laura probably didn't notice the tight set in her mother's jaw as she came forward to help Presley. That, or she chalked it up to being upset that her daughter was hurt.

"Mom, you remember Laura. She took me to the emergency room."

"It's good to see you again, Mrs. Royale. I wish it was under better circumstances."

Katerina Royale offered Laura a tight smile and nod. "Thank you for helping Presley."

Her mother took the crutches from Laura and offered her hand to Presley in a clear *I'll take it from here* gesture meant to dismiss Laura.

"How long will you be off it, Pres? I'll call Timothy and have him get you on a rehab schedule."

Of course she would.

Presley clamped down on the urge to tell her mom she didn't need the physical therapist to come to the house immediately, but that would be foolish. If they were going to get her back on the circuit with as few shows missed as possible, they needed to start therapy right away.

She turned to Laura. "Thank you so much, Laura. I'll call you guys in a few days."

Laura leaned in to hug Presley. "Cade will ride Tess for you. You just take care and get some rest."

"Thank you." Presley had said it already, but she said it again. Cade rode Tess for Presley when she was out on the circuit, but she always made sure she got over there between shows. She wouldn't be able to ride Tess at all for the time being.

Laura knew Presley didn't live the life of a normal thirty-year-old woman. None of her life had been normal.

Presley Royale had been put on a horse's back before she could walk. The first time she went over a jump, she flew over it without any hesitation. Or so she was told. She didn't remember the event, but her father liked to tell people it never entered her mind that the horse might refuse the jump and send her flying over it instead.

Now, at thirty, she lived in the in-law suite of her parents' home. She traveled more days of the year than she was home, and her world was ruled by the demands of her career in Grand Prix show jumping.

What she ate, who she was friends with, her schedule, all of it.

It was only in the last few years that she'd started to want something different in her world, but how could she give up and walk away?

Her mother helped her into the house, calling out to the housekeeper to help as they entered.

"We'll get you settled in the living room." Mrs. Royale had already let go of Presley and picked up her phone, leaving Presley to lean on her crutches again.

Presley didn't have to ask who she was texting. Really, it was only an issue of who would be first. Her physical therapist or her dad. Either way, both would arrive quickly. One would demand answers.

"Honestly, Presley, I don't know why you can't see that keeping that horse at that barn is a bad idea."

Her mother's words were the polite version of what her father would say when he came. Rather than sell Tess when it had been time to retire her, Presley had insisted on buying her from Royale Stables so she could keep her.

Tess was the only horse in the constantly rotating string of horses Presley rode in the circuit that she had always felt was truly hers. Tess was the only horse Presley had found on her own, without any help from her dad. When Presley was sixteen, she'd chosen Tess when the horse was only six years old, long before she would be ready for the Grand Prix level. She'd trained her, brought her up to being one of the best in the country.

When Tess had been ready to step down from the Grand Prix level, Presley had bought her, but her father refused to let her keep Tess at Royale Stables. If she wasn't making him money, she wasn't earning her keep. Never mind that Presley offered to pay the horse's feed and board. That wasn't the way it worked, he'd told her.

He hadn't needed to tell her. Presley knew that wasn't the way her father worked. If he hadn't sanctioned something, it wasn't going to happen on his land. She wouldn't dream of pointing out that the land, stables, and house belonged to her mother.

She didn't other to argue with her mother about keeping Tess on their land. Her mother knew her father wouldn't let her keep Tess on their property. She certainly hadn't insisted her father let her, even though the land was all technically her mother's.

"The accident had nothing to do with where Tess is

boarded, mom. It was a snake. Tess spooked then stumbled."
She shrugged. Her mother knew enough about horses to fill
in the rest.

Her mother had once been her father's student, back
when he was starting out as a young trainer. Horse trainers
rarely owned their own property or the kind of horses her
dad now owned. They were hired to train riders who
wanted to show on either their own horses or horses they'd
leased.

But her father had fallen for her mother, a rider who'd
competed at almost the level Presley was at now. When
they married, Katerina Dudikoff's family fortune was more
than enough to buy him any land he chose and any horses
he set his sights on. Katerina had helped him build his
training career, with herself at the center of it as his prized
student. When he'd built his reputation and could hand
pick who he worked with, she'd retired from the circuit,
preferring the parties and events from the viewer's side of
things instead of the saddle side. Being the wife of a
famous trainer and the mother of a famous rider suited
Katerina.

Her mother didn't give up. "It had everything to do with
that horse and that stable." She let out a delicate sniff. "Not
that it could really be called a stable."

"It's a stable, mother," Presley said, as the housekeeper
propped pillows under her leg and behind her back on the
couch.

"If it was a proper stable, they wouldn't have snakes."

Presley didn't argue. There was little point in letting her
mother know that their own stables occasionally had snakes.
It was impossible not to. Sure, you could sprinkle products
meant to keep them away, but one or two would turn up
now and then, regardless.

Her father's voice came from the doorway, and it wasn't cheerful. "How long?"

She knew what he meant. How long would she be out? How many shows would she miss? Would it be enough to affect her standing?

"Four weeks," Presley said, knowing he'd rail no matter the answer. It could easily have been six or eight, if the sprain had been worse.

"We'll see what Timothy has to say," her mother said.

"The doctor said four," Presley said. She wasn't going to let them force her back before she was ready. There was a time when Presley cared as much about her career as her parents did. She'd have been pushing to shave time off as much as they would, but those days were over.

She'd started to think she didn't want to do this forever. She just hadn't found a way to tell her parents she wanted to retire.

Her father stood stone-faced in the door until the house-keeper slipped from the room. His anger was never the loud kind. He had a way of icing himself over that was scary to a kid and intimidating as hell to most adults. Presley still hated it, even though she'd been an adult for years.

"This was foolish, Presley. You're putting everything we've worked for at risk every time you go over there and ride that nag."

Presley wanted to laugh. It was ridiculous to call Tess a nag. She might not be able to compete at the Grand Prix level any longer, but if Presley hadn't wanted to keep her, they could have easily sold her to someone wanting to compete at lower levels or in a different discipline. Never mind the fact that he'd charged Presley twenty-five-thousand dollars to buy Tess when she retired.

She didn't laugh. She simply waited him out as he

lectured her on what her carelessness might mean to her career. She wondered what he would do. Her parents weren't ever abusive, but her father did have a mean streak and he could be passive-aggressive when he wanted to.

Growing up, she'd seen that early on. Anyone in the riding world knew horses weren't pets. You didn't get to retire your horses to live out their lives on a pasture on your land, even when you had as much land as they had. Each year, they assessed the string of three to five horses she was competing with and made decisions about which to keep or sell.

Of course, her father seemed to put a little something into the analysis at times. Her first pony had been sold after a particularly bad showing. He'd said it was time for her to start riding a larger pony, but she'd known, even then, that he used the timing to make a statement to her. To teach her what could happen if she didn't meet his expectations.

Other times, he'd take on a new student. One time, when Presley had told him she was afraid to try a jump he wanted her to take, he'd only waited a week before signing on with a girl who had teased Presley mercilessly at previous shows. The girl had been the first one to dub Presley "the Royale Princess," and the name hadn't been used in a complimentary sense.

He never had to tell her why he was doing what he did. She was always able to look back and know just where she'd messed up.

Of course, as she got older, it was harder for him to hurt her in those ways. She'd gotten to the point where she didn't care as much who he took on to train, and she'd made sure she didn't get attached to any of the horses. With the exception of Tess, that is.

Actually, it was a miracle he'd never sold her over the

years. Maybe her mother had stopped him. Who knew? It was never very clear to Presley how much control her mother exerted, but Presley had a feeling her mother still manipulated the purse strings. Katerina wasn't one to give up control.

It was no matter. Presley owned Tess outright now and her father couldn't do anything to Presley that she wouldn't be able to get over. No matter how much she still craved his approval, she had learned to harden herself to his particular brand of retribution.

She tuned back in to hear her father telling her to withdraw her entries for the next three weeks before he stalked out of the room.

She would withdraw for four and then see how her ankle was.

Presley lay her head back and closed her eyes. She'd been planning her retirement for some time now, but hadn't quite known how to actually go through with it. She knew what she wanted to do afterward. She had a business chosen, her plan drafted. She had a life planned for after her exit from the circuit, one that didn't involve going into the training business the way she was sure a lot of people thought she might. Maybe it was time for her to live that dream. *Her* dream.

She heard a rustle and opened her eyes to see her mother settling herself on the ottoman near the couch.

Her mom took her hand and pressed her lips together a moment before speaking. "He loves you, you know? We both do."

"I know, Mom. I do." As hard as her father could be, she'd felt his pride when she did well. Even earning an "atta girl" or "well done," was high praise, for most of his riders, but he'd given her those often. He would squeeze her leg as he walked beside her horse and when she looked down and grinned at him, he'd wink up at her.

With her dad, it was little things like that. Little things he never offered his other students.

Her mother took one of her hands and pressed it between both of her own, rubbing as if she needed to warm her. "I'll take care of the withdrawals for you. You need to rest. Do you want me to get you some tea or a little lunch?"

And just like that, Presley began to question her resolve. How could she walk away from all her parents had done for her? They'd given her everything every little girl ever wanted. Horses, ponies, and a life anyone would kill to have.

CHAPTER THREE

James told himself he was just taking a break. Splitting logs the size of the ones he was working with was labor intensive. It wasn't why he'd stopped, though. He'd stopped because Presley had just limped up to where Tess stood at a pasture fence. He'd heard through Laura that the ankle had just been sprained but even that would mean a month or more out of the saddle. He hoped she wasn't planning to ride.

He heard the soft crunch of someone approaching him from behind. He had to slow his turn in a conscious effort to defeat the demons that urged him to spin and watch his back. He was on Bishop Ranch. He wasn't in a deep dark hole where someone might beat him as he slept for no other reason than the sheer entertainment of seeing if they could break the American. If they could break *the Illusion*, as he'd been called at times.

James found Laura watching him as she approached, but her eyes quickly slid past his shoulder to where Presley stood in the back paddock. When her eyes found him again, there was worry there.

"She's complicated, James."

James didn't answer. He didn't have anything to say. He could object and tell her he'd been avoiding Presley like the plague, even going up to his loft when she came to look for him. Which, she had the other day, leaving him a box of cinnamon buns and a thank you note for his help when she'd hurt her ankle.

"You're complicated," Laura said, adding to the pile of reasons to stay away from Presley. As though he needed a pile bigger than the one he'd already stacked up in his head. Presley didn't need him in her life. No woman did.

Laura looked to the tree trunks he was splitting. "New project?"

"Yeah." He lifted the iron wedge and sledge hammer and readied the wedge for the next split.

"What are you making?"

"Work table. For your greenhouse."

She rewarded him with a smile that lit her face. "For me?"

He nodded. "I haven't decided yet what it will look like." He ran a hand over the bark. "This bark is nice, so I might make that the table top, set it in some resin to give you a flat surface. You'd still be able to see the bark through the resin. Or I could flip them and let the bark be visible on the underside and sides of the table."

"It will be gorgeous," she said. She'd always had more faith in him than she should.

"YOU'RE NOT THINKING of getting on, are you?"

Presley turned to grin at Cade. "No, I'm not that crazy."

"Laura said four weeks?" Cade asked.

"Yes. At least." Presley didn't mention that her physical therapist thought he could get her there sooner. "I really appreciate you adding extra rides to your schedule for her. Just add them to my boarding bill."

"Actually, I wanted to talk to you about that." Cade stepped up onto the railing next to her. "How would you feel about letting James ride her?"

Presley looked to the brother barn. "James? Can he ride?"

Cade nodded. "He can. Worked at a stable when he was in high school and rode there quite a bit. He wouldn't jump her or anything."

Presley chewed on her lip and looked at Tess, who'd moved away a short distance to tug at young tufts of grass just outside the fence line. She didn't want to take a chance on someone who wasn't skilled enough riding Tess, but she also didn't want to say no. If Cade was asking, that must mean he didn't have the time to ride her himself. Maybe she could get a friend to come over. Someone she knew was up to riding Tess.

Now Cade was looking over at the barn where James likely was. "If you aren't comfortable with it, I understand, but I wouldn't ask if I didn't think he had the skill. I promise you. I've asked Laura and he used to handle some tough horses where he rode. It's just that, I was hoping to tell him I needed the help."

"You don't?" Presley asked.

"No. I can ride her if you need me to. It's just that I thought getting out of the barn might be good for James. He's got Lulu in there with him, but he needs something to draw him out. A horse would be good therapy for him."

It made perfect sense. Horses were good therapy both mentally and physically.

Presley looked out to the barn again and nodded. If it could help James, and Cade was sure he had the skill, she couldn't say no. Besides, she trusted Cade. He'd never let someone ride her horse who didn't know what they were doing.

"Will you be here the first time he gets on?" She would have insisted she be there the first time, but something told her that wouldn't be a good idea for James.

"Absolutely."

"Then I hope Tess can help him." She meant it. After all James had been through, he deserved every chance he had at living a life free of whatever demons haunted him. She had a feeling they were many.

CHAPTER FOUR

James stood at the window of the loft, looking out at the black landscape. The window had been the hay door to the barn at one point, but they'd framed it out and installed glass when they redid the space for him.

He liked the quiet of the ranch after everyone had gone to bed for the night. He'd eventually lay down and try to sleep, but not before he wore himself out as much as he could. He moved back a few steps, then reached above him for the bar that went from one ceiling beam to another.

One, two, three, four...

He liked getting lost in the mindlessness of the counting as he pulled his body up over the bar again and again.

Ten, eleven, twelve ...

With any luck, he'd be able to fall asleep before midnight.

He dropped to the ground when a set of headlights pulled up the long drive that led into the ranch. Drawn back to the window, he watched as the truck slowed near the stables where Cade and Presley kept their horses and any other animals Cade was rehabbing at the time. His brother-in-law was a whiz where animals were concerned, taking in ponies and horses to rehab and sell. He also took in any number of other breeds. Everything from rats from the local rat rescue, to goats that had been mistreated and needed a calm hand.

The truck stopped and James watched as the door opened and a figure stepped out.

That was all it took for him to recognize the man. It was a silhouette he'd seen time and time again in the dark. The tall lanky build was hard to miss, even though James hadn't expected to see his former squad mate in Texas.

"Hunt," he said under his breath, then grabbed a shirt to tug on and hoofed it down the steps to the loft, Lulu on his heels.

He came around his barn in time to see Hunt walking around to the doors of the stable, looking for a way in.

James gave a sharp whistle and raised his arm above his head when Jeff's head came up.

As Jeff Hunt hiked it to where James waited for him, James let the memories hit him like bricks. He knew they'd hurt coming at him, but the faster he let them hit, the faster he'd get the pain over with.

"What the hell? Just passing through Texas?" He asked as Jeff clasped his hand and arm in a tight grip.

White teeth flashed. "Went so many years without being able to check on your scrawny ass, thought I'd check in."

James gave him the kind of look that said he could have used the phone.

"Cool place," Hunt said as James led them back through the darkened space of the barn and up to the loft.

"It works." James was more than grateful for the quiet place to come to after he'd finished his treatment and debriefing. He just wasn't one to gush over the décor. Hunt, on the other hand, liked to gush. He'd been the guy who always had something positive to look at, even when they'd been in the pits of hell. It was a mystery how he did it.

He'd last seen Hunt in the hospital when he and Eric Larson—known in their squad as Lars because of his name and his Nordic good looks—had shown up within days of his arrival.

Learning that only two members of his squad had made it out of the firefight had been a blow. He had no memory of the firefight that left him in captivity for years.

It might have been a blessing now that he knew the whole squad, save the three of them, had been wiped out. Thirteen men lost in a massacre.

"Drink?" James tilted a water bottle at Hunt. "Or I have beer. Or milk. I've got milk." Milk was one of the things he'd craved since getting out. He hadn't craved anything when he was in captivity. Hadn't allowed it. It would have killed him to want anything in that hellhole.

Now, he could indulge a craving for days. Last week, he'd eaten nothing but giant bowls of Rice Krispies cereal with sugar sprinkled on it. Bowl after bowl. The week before that, it had been Hot dogs and potato chips. The sour cream and onion kind.

"Beer." Hunt grunted the response, like James should have known he'd choose a beer over milk or water any day.

James returned the water to the fridge and pulled out two longneck beers, pausing to open them before turning back to Hunt.

The tilt that hit him when he saw Hunt's boots as he turned caught him off guard and he froze for a minute, grasping at the strands of memory that tickled his mind. A flash of boots on the ground. Stacks of crates. Weapons.

It was a millisecond's hesitation at best, but Hunt caught it.

"What?"

"You ever feel like there was something off in that last mission?" He didn't know how to put his doubts to words.

Shadows crossed his friend's face. "There was a lot that was off that night, but why don't you tell me what you mean?"

James shook his head, reaching to hand Hunt the beer then falling into one of the two large chairs that took up residence in one corner of the open studio space. "It's not something I can point to specifically. There's something I keep trying to remember, but I don't know what it is. It feels important, though. And it feels wrong, like there's something I'm not going to want to know once I do remember it."

Hunt sat in the other chair and Lulu flopped down at James's feet, letting one paw rest on James's bare foot.

Hunt looked at James, and for once, the strong facade Hunt kept up fell. "I think maybe it's a good thing you can't remember that night. It might not be a bad thing to just let it go."

James didn't answer. He'd been telling himself that for a while now, but something kept trying to break through. He wasn't able to shut it out.

"Nice dog."

James let his hand fall to pet Lulu's head. "Thanks. My brother-in-law trained her for me. I guess he does a lot of that sort of thing."

"Trained her for what?"

James took a long pull on the beer before answering. "She does things for me. Wakes me up if I have a nightmare. If I have a panic attack, she seems to know before I even know it's happening. She recognizes signs of agitation, like if I'm clenching my fists. She'll interrupt that."

In reality, there was more the dog did for him. Some of it, Cade had told him, couldn't be trained. A dog either had an aptitude for it or not. Lulu seemed to sense when he was having trouble. She'd climb right into his lap sometimes and just sit there for hours like she knew he needed an anchor or something.

Cade called it an embrace behavior, but all James knew was she'd let him cling to her like she was his life float. In some ways, she was.

"Does he do that for a living? Your brother-in-law, I mean."

"Not really. His family has money so he doesn't need to work, but he rescues animals, rehabs them and stuff. Knows a lot about training. I guess when he heard I was coming, he started looking for a dog he could train for me."

Hunt nodded and looked down at the bottle in his hands. "I've heard there's a long wait for most service dogs like that."

"I think there is." It felt like Hunt wasn't saying something. "You think you need one?"

Hunt shook his head. "Not me. Lars."

"He's struggling?" None of them liked to talk about any of this shit, but he owed Lars and Hunt. Even though, in the end, it had been a lot of people coming together to get him out of South America, he knew Lars and Hunt had never stopped pushing the Army for him. They'd thought they were pushing for the military to go in and find his remains and bring them out. They hadn't held out hope he could be alive, but still, they'd been there for him when no one even knew he'd survived the firefight.

He thought of the scarring and burns running up his

legs. He'd been lucky. His were second degree burns so they scarred and had taken months to heal, but they hadn't done significant damage to the nerves in his legs or to any of the joints or bones.

Whenever he thought of the months of healing his body had required, thoughts of Catalina tried to push to the forefront of his mind, but he didn't let them. Thinking of her was more than he was ready for.

Hunt answered slowly, as though he didn't want to put words to what was happening. "He's drinking a lot. Last time I went to see him, he started hurling shit at me, told me to get out. I know Izzy's been trying to get him to go see someone, but he's fighting her on it."

Izzy married Lars before he went overseas. They had two beautiful little girls together. James couldn't remember how old the girls would be now, but the oldest couldn't be more than seven or eight.

"You've talked to Izzy?"

"Yeah. She says it's bad. She's worried about the girls. He's angry all the time. He used to have wild mood swings, but she said now he stays on the angry side of things most of the time. She's going to take the girls to her mom's house in Vermont for a while."

Hunt and Lars were both living in Pennsylvania.

"I can ask Cade if he can train a dog for Lars, but it'll take a few months, at least, I think. We can ask him in the morning."

Hunt nodded. "Maybe I can get him to talk to someone in the meantime."

James knew Hunt would try. Hunt had taken on responsibility for both James and Lars.

"How long you plan to stay?" James asked. He liked the idea of getting to spend a few days with Hunt. It was different being around people who knew what you'd been through. Who understood you without having to talk about it. On the other hand, the longer Hunt stayed, the more he might see that James wasn't doing all that great. He still hadn't set foot off the ranch since he got here, and the thought of doing that terrified him. He didn't want to lay any more guilt at Hunt's feet so he sure as hell wouldn't let on to any of that.

"Couple days. I have to get back to work and I want to stay close to Lars."

James nodded. "What are you doing for work these days?"

"Private security. You remember Dylan O'Leary?"

"Vaguely." James remembered the name well enough to know they'd been through basic together, but they'd lost touch after that.

"He's got a company. It's small. Just a few of us. We do security at private events, the occasional bodyguard shit. Nothing major. It's all pretty low key, but I like that."

James could see that for Hunt. A lot of guys who left the service wanted to find a way to stay in the game. Maybe it was the adrenaline. Maybe it was because they didn't know anything else. Hunt had never seemed the type.

They spent another hour talking about a whole lot of nothing before Hunt crashed on the couch and James did his best to catch a few hours of sleep before the nightmares kicked in. With Lulu curled up next to him on the bed, he almost felt like he could ward them off. Almost.

CHAPTER FIVE

They found Cade first thing, sitting at his mother's breakfast table. James didn't spend a lot of time at May Bishop's
house, but she'd told him he was welcome anytime.

James made the introductions, including Josh, May
Bishop's live-in boyfriend. Laura had told him Josh was an
old friend of the family, and he'd been responsible for
getting her to the ranch when she was hiding from her
deceased husband's family.

Laura's daughter, Jamie, who was now three-years-old
but seemed more like a teenager some days, launched
herself at James. He held her, breathing in the scent of her.
He didn't spend a lot of time with her. Truth was, he was a
little afraid one of his flashbacks would hit when he was
with her and he'd scare the hell out of her. But when he did
see her, it was like getting to hold a little piece of heaven in
his arms. The girl was pure love, pure joy.

James set Jamie down and she ran back to Josh's side,
digging into her pancakes.

"Eat, boys," May said, ignoring the fact she was talking
to four quite grown-up men. She put plates on the table and

bowls and platters with pancakes and scrambled eggs appeared in short order.

Hunt and James competed to see who could put away the most food in the shortest time. Even James had to admit he should be taking May up on her offer to feed him more often.

"Cade, how long does it take to train a dog like Lulu?" James asked.

Cade finished chewing a bite of biscuit and gravy before answering. "Anywhere from eight to eighteen months. I was lucky with Lulu. One of my friends had her halfway trained on some other stuff before we found out you'd be coming. I was able to finish off her training in a pretty short time because of that, but usually it takes time to find and evaluate the dogs, then at least eight months or more for the training."

James wondered if he'd thanked his brother-in-law properly for what he'd done for him. Cade's whole family had been there for him from the day he came home, no expectations of anything in return. They'd treated him like he was their blood, even though the family connection was only through marriage.

"You need a dog?" Cade asked Hunt, not seeming bothered by the fact that they might ask him to train another dog for free.

"Not me. Our buddy, Lars."

Cade wiped his mouth and thanked his mother for the food, then rose and cleared the plates from the table. James and Hunt rose and helped with the job.

"Let's go out to the stables," Cade said, leading the way out the back door of the kitchen.

Hunt stopped and looked to the wheelchair on the porch and the paved sidewalks that went from the house to both of the barns and even out into some of the fields on the property.

"My mom," Cade said, answering the unspoken question. "She gets around inside the house most of the time without her chair, but she can't walk for very long without it. We've set up the ranch so she can get around in her chair."

They continued down the path as Cade asked questions about Lars. "Does he have any physical disabilities?"

"No," Hunt said, and James knew it was a bit of a miracle the guy didn't. Hunt walked with a heavy limp and James was sure he and Lars both had their share of pain, but they had their limbs and senses intact.

"PTSD or TBI diagnosis?" Cade asked. PTSD stood for post-traumatic stress disorder, although James knew the facility he'd been in while he healed now referred to it as PTSS, for post-traumatic stress syndrome. TBI stood for traumatic brain injury.

"Both," Hunt said, and James shot him a look. He didn't know about the TBI, but he supposed he should have realized it was a possibility with what Hunt had told him. "He's having a lot of anger issues."

Cade looked grim but led them into the barn. "You're going to need to get him some help while I work on the dog. If his anger issues are severe, we have to think of the safety and well-being of the dog when we pair them. I can train the dog to handle yelling and even some throwing things and stuff, but I need to know the dog is safe from harm. Can you convince your friend to see someone if he knows there's a dog coming to him down the road?"

"I can try," was all Hunt could offer.

"I'll call around to some of the trainers in the area and see if anyone has a lead on a good candidate. Sometimes, they'll be training a dog for one thing like search and rescue or detection work, and the dog washes out but would be a good candidate for another type of work. Other times, they might know of a dog someone needs to re-home who might work. I can also touch base with the rescues and shelters I work with and see if they have any dogs I can test. I got Lulu from a friend who planned to use her for search and rescue work, but she wasn't taking to it as much as he'd have liked. He let me repurpose her for James."

He looked to Hunt. "I can train the dog up as fast as possible, but you're still looking at months of wait time. And I'll need him to come here to work with me and the dog for a bit when the dog is ready. Can he do that?"

Hunt didn't hesitate. "I'll get him here. Hopefully, just knowing there's help coming might be enough to get him through until you can get a dog ready for him. But listen, I don't know how much money we can scrape together for this. I know this has probably got to cost you—"

Cade didn't let him finish. He waved off the words. "I don't need any payment." He turned to James. "But I do need something from you. You can consider it payment for the dog."

The muscles in James's stomach clenched. He had a feeling Cade was going to ask him to spend more time with Laura. How could he tell him he couldn't look at his sister without feeling the guilt of knowing he'd left her in the hands of a monster for years?

They stopped in front of Tess's stall and the mare poked her head out looking to see who her visitors were, probably wondering if they had anything to offer her. Cade slipped a peppermint from his pocket, unwrapped it and offered it to the horse.

Hunt laughed. "Mints? Is that normal?"

Cade grinned. "Yeah. My wife tries to get me to feed them carrots, but they still like mints now and again." He turned to James. "I need you to ride Tess for me while Presley's out with her sprained ankle. You don't need to jump her or anything, but if you can hop on her for a little while three or four days a week, I can jump her once a week."

James looked to the mare. He hadn't thought about getting back on a horse. It had been years since he'd worked at a riding stable and it wasn't something he gave much thought to anymore. Now that Cade had stuck the idea in his head, though, he had to say it wasn't a bad one.

"Presley doesn't mind if I ride her?" He had seen first-hand that Presley Royale loved the horse. He had no doubts about his ability to handle the mare, but he would have thought he'd need to prove that to her before she'd let him near Tess.

"I ran it by her and she's okay with it as long as I watch you the first couple of times."

James looked to the horse, then to Cade, then back to the horse.

It would mean venturing out of the barn each day, and that wasn't something he was looking forward to. It wasn't like he would run into a lot of people on the ranch, but he'd certainly see more of his sister and Cade, and probably even May and Josh. Then again, being out this morning hadn't been so horrible.

He looked down to where Lulu stood by his side. The truth was, Lars needed that dog. James also owed Cade. A lot. No way in hell he'd say no to anything Cade asked of him.

CHAPTER SIX

Presley stayed away for three days, long enough for Cade to text and let her know James had been up on Tess twice and was handling her beautifully. Of course, it hadn't been hard to stay away during that time since she'd been busy on the circuit.

Despite being hurt, she was expected to attend any local shows with Grand Prix level classes. It had been a rule her father established early on. You spent your time recuperating with the physical therapist and studying your competition.

She'd been glad for the rule this time. Of course, she often spent time at competitions watching the other competitors from the sidelines, but it was different when you didn't have to keep track of when you needed to warm up and what was happening with your mount, or any other concerns while you watched.

Now, though, she had four days of down time and she planned to spend some of that at the barn with Tess, even though she wouldn't be the one riding her.

She spotted James and Tess in the outdoor ring immediately. Of course, he was every bit as strong a rider as Cade said he'd be. Tess tried the little playful dance she did when she was warming up, but James's steady hands drew the mare back under the bit.

Presley moved to a large log and sat watching from a distance. She didn't want to distract horse or rider. Of course, Tess would notice her pretty soon, but until then, she would watch.

Watching wasn't a hardship where James Lawless was involved. She knew she shouldn't think those things, but hey, as long as she only thought them and never acted on them, there wasn't really any harm.

Maybe.

She cringed. She sounded awful in her own head, but really, she couldn't help but notice the man's long, lean muscles or the way his body flexed with power as he rode.

She didn't know quite where the thoughts had come from. She'd watched many men in the ring and, of course, over the years she'd had a crush here and there. There was something different, though, about watching someone decked out in the stiff coat and britches of the show arena.

There was nothing stiff about James. He wore a pair of jeans that looked like they'd been cut to his fit with just the right amount of stretch in all the right places. And his t-shirt stretched over back muscles that weren't like any she'd noticed through a hunt coat.

His arms were muscular, but not tan, she noticed. And it made sense. She hadn't seen him outside much. She wondered if Cade's plan would help him. Surely getting outside and interacting with Tess each day would help. She'd always thought horses were soothing to the soul.

Tess threw up her head and turned to cut across the ring toward Presley, and she knew she'd been spotted. She rose, coming forward through the short grass, moving slowly on the air cast that still encased her ankle.

James gave up trying to turn Tess back as soon as he saw Presley.

She was surprised to see a smile cross his face and wondered for a brief second if he knew he'd even made the gesture.

"You look great up there," Presley said, then flushed as she heard her own words. "I mean, she looks like she's going well for you."

Wow, she sounded like an idiot.

If he noticed, he didn't say. He leaned over and patted Tess's neck as Tess came to the rail to greet Presley.

"Thanks," he said. "She's a great ride."

Oh Lord. Presley shut out the thoughts that ran through her head at that one. The horse, he was talking about the horse.

His grin told her he knew what her mind had done with his words.

The moment could have turned tense, but a man with a heavy limp joined them. Tall and lanky with the kind of short hair that said he had been in the military at one time or maybe still was. Either that, or he admired the haircuts given in the army.

"My day is looking up," the man said as he dropped a duffel bag by his feet and offered a hand to Presley. "I woke up with this guy, so you're a sight for sore eyes. I'm Jeff Hunt."

"Presley Royale," she said as she took his hand.

He winked at her, holding her hand a little longer than what was polite, but there was a playfulness to his gesture. If she wasn't mistaken, the playfulness was directed as much at James as it was at her.

James didn't seem to get the joke. He dropped down off Tess, holding onto her reins, but moving closer to Presley, even though they stood on opposite sides of the fence.

"Don't you need to be getting on the road, Hunt?"

Hunt only laughed, making Presley smile. She couldn't help it. The joking felt good. And the fact that James seemed to care if his friend flirted with her felt better.

The smile Hunt turned on her was pure sin. It was probably one that should have done something to her, but it didn't. Still, Presley had to admit, she liked the attention. She didn't get that much in her life.

She hadn't gone to school. She'd been taught by tutors. On the circuit, she was always Lawrence Royale's daughter. Always was and always would be. The boys who had hit on her as a teen and the men who hit on her now had other reasons for wanting her. It wasn't ever about her. It was about what her family or her father could do for them.

There had been a boy she thought was interested in her when she was seventeen. Not her dad, not her mom, not the family name or the family stables.

She'd had two weeks of feeling butterflies in her stomach whenever he came around, whenever he turned his smile her way. When he grabbed her hand while they cooled down their horses.

Two weeks. Her dad had chased him off. Actually, he'd done more than just chase the kid off. Joseph Andrighetti's parents had been told they would either get their son under control or they were going to find their son and his horse weren't welcome on any trainer's roster or in any stable in the area.

Presley wasn't really sure her dad had the power to do that. But it didn't matter. Joseph's parents must have believed it. What really hurt was how easily Joseph had been chased away. Presley had been so sure he wouldn't be swayed by anything her father said. She was so sure he would laugh and tell her no one could change the way he felt about her.

Seventeen-year-olds were stupid that way.

Then again, it had happened with Chris Anderly when she was twenty-seven, so maybe she hadn't outgrown that particular stupidity.

Well, the Chris thing hadn't been exactly like the Joseph thing. With Chris, she'd believed he was interested in her, believed he couldn't possibly want anything from her dad or her family name because he'd been so high up in the ranks of competitors, had a trainer he liked, and had money of his own.

She shook her head, not wanting to relive the moment she'd found out one of those things wasn't true. Hearing him on the phone with another woman had been a shock. Finding out he'd lost all of his money to a scam investment and needed her if he was going to keep living his life the way he wanted to had been devastating.

Presley tuned back in to find James and Hunt saying their goodbyes.

Hunt rested one fist on James's shoulder. "I'll call when I get in."

James looked almost apologetic. "Listen, maybe I can go with you," he started, but Hunt was shaking his head.

"No way, brother, you got shit you need to do here. You just take care of you for now, you hear me?"

There was a thick tension in the air and Presley felt almost like an intruder. In a move that went against everything she typically did, she found herself trying to break the tension instead of surreptitiously move away from the private conversation.

"Wow, I think you guys just reenacted a scene from *Pretty Woman*."

Hunt and James looked at her for a minute before Hunt winked and sauntered closer. "I can reenact all the *Pretty Woman* you want."

He didn't get closer. James reached over the fence, grabbed him by the back of his shirt and tugged, hard, bringing an unrepentant grin to Hunt's face.

"You're done, Romeo. Call me when you get in." With that, James shoved Hunt toward his waiting truck and moved back to Presley's side.

JAMES WATCHED as Hunt turned his truck in a tight K turn before heading down the drive with one arm waving out the window.

He still felt like he should be going with him, like he owed it to Lars to help him, but the truth was, he hadn't left the ranch since he'd come to it. He wasn't sure he wouldn't just slow Hunt down. If he started having panic attacks on the road...

Having Lulu with him helped a hell of a lot, but still, it was one thing riding a horse on the ranch. It was quite another going out and dealing with the real world.

"You okay?" Presley asked quietly beside him.

He turned to look her way, seeing deep blue eyes staring back at him. He expected to feel like a bug being examined under a microscope. Or that he'd see pity there. He didn't. All he saw was concern and he realized that was a different thing than pity.

He nodded and took the reins from her. "I'll cool her down," he said.

As he said it, he realized he hoped she would hang around afterward while he brushed Tess in the barn. Presley had made him laugh and smile more in one day than he had in a long time. That meant something. In fact, he thought, as she watched him walk Tess, that meant a whole hell of a lot.

CHAPTER SEVEN

"You probably can't wait to get back on her, huh? You're missing a month of shows, right?" James asked as he ran the curry comb in circles over Tess's back.

"Yes and no," she said.

James looked at her, waiting for her to say more.

She did. "I can't wait to get back up on Tess, but I'm okay with missing the shows."

"Really?" He hadn't expected that. He would have thought she'd be upset to be missing so many shows. From the little he knew of Presley, show jumping was her life. As he looked at her now, he saw she looked a little surprised by her own admission.

She was slow to answer. "I guess I've just been a little ready to slow down."

"I didn't know there was such a thing in show jumping. At least not at your level." The barn he'd worked at when he was in high school had been on the east coast and it had definitely had its share of competitive riders in jumpers, hunters, and equitation. There had even been a couple of big dressage riders. From what he remembered, it was intense.

She had her lips pressed tightly together as she stared at a spot on the wall, as though she was trying to work something through in her own mind before answering.

"I guess I just don't love it as much as I used to. The riding—that part, I love. I still love that feeling that you're flying when you go over a jump and the feeling of partnering with a good horse. But I just," she fluttered her hands in the air like she was looking for words to bring her thoughts to fruition, "I don't know. I guess my heart isn't into the competition any more."

"Was it ever?" He asked, switching the circular strokes of the curry comb for the short brisk strokes of the hard brush that would take off the dirt the curry had loosened.

Now she looked at him with surprise and he liked that she appeared to be thinking before answering him. It meant she was probably telling him the truth instead of giving him an off-the-cuff answer that would satisfy his questions without really telling him anything.

"My career has always been tightly tied to my relationship with my parents," she said slowly, then seemed to rush to correct a perceived slight. "Don't get me wrong, I love my parents. And I've loved the life they've given me even if it was unconventional. I just think I've loved the feeling of competing and winning because when I'm competing and winning, my parents are happy."

"And is that enough anymore?" He sounded like a therapist, but whatever. He didn't care. He genuinely wanted to hear the answer. He'd wondered why she kept her retired horse at Cade's instead of on her parents' land. Surely, they had room for one retired horse there.

She quirked her head at him. "I think so." Now a frown. "Maybe."

The words "maybe not" slid through his mind, but he clamped down on them before they could come out of his mouth. It wasn't his place to tell her what to do. Instead, he settled for, "If you weren't riding, what would you be doing?"

Her mouth opened quickly, but he could see her deliberately slow her response. "I've thought of opening a florist shop."

"Really?" That wasn't at all what he would have guessed.

She laughed at his surprise. "Yeah, it's a little silly, really. I asked myself what I would do if I wasn't riding a couple of years ago, and I realized I would enjoy owning a business. A lot of people think I would train other riders or maybe breed and train horses or something, but I guess I realized I don't really want to do that. I started looking at what I might do."

"And?" He asked, moving on to the soft brush that would finish off the coat.

"And, I researched options."

That made him laugh. Leave it to Presley to research things instead of going with her gut interests.

She seemed to like his laughter, answering with a cheeky grin. "I like research, so I looked up businesses that can thrive in a small town—"

"Because you want to stay in Evers?"

She glanced up at that and nodded. "Yeah, I do."

He didn't know much about Evers. He had yet to step foot into the town. Although, if he thought about it, he did know something about the town. As soon as the people of this town found out he was coming, they'd come out to the ranch to help Cade and his brother, Shane, turn the loft into an apartment for him. That said a hell of a lot for the people of the town.

And even though he had to guess plenty of people were talking about him in town, speculating about the man who had been captured by the enemy and held captive for five years, none of them had shown up on the ranch trying to snoop into his business.

That said even more about the people in the town.

"So you researched small town businesses. What else?" He asked. He rubbed his hand over the spot between Tess's eyes that always made her lean into him and then unhooked the cross-ties so he could lead her into her stall. She knew he'd filled a bucket with grain and had it waiting in her stall. She turned immediately to the open door and hurried to the bucket, not caring in the least that he followed behind her to close and latch the door.

He joined Presley on the large tack trunk she had taken up residence on and settled in beside her, one of his legs resting slightly against hers. He shouldn't like the contact so much, but he did.

"I looked at the list of businesses that gave me and then looked at what I thought I would be good at. For one thing, I don't love talking to people."

"Really?" She always seemed downright chatty to him, but maybe that was because he didn't talk much. Maybe it was only her in comparison to him that made her seem talkative.

She shrugged. "I don't mind talking to people for a short time, but I don't like having to hold a big conversation, I guess. And I don't like crowds. My family hosts a lot of events. I hate them. You have to spend the entire time talking to people and trying to remember who they are or how they're connected to your parents. You know?"

He grinned and shook his head. "Not at all."

"Well, take my word for it. It makes me break out in hives."

"Okay, so small town business and not talking a lot to people left flower shop?"

She nodded, and he realized he could smell the light scent of her as they sat. He didn't know if it was her shampoo or her soap or just something innate to her.

He stood and went to lean on the wall on the opposite side of the aisle. It had been a mistake to sit so close to her.

"It left that and a couple of other things. I chose flower shop in the end because I love flowers and I realized I would be good at it. I like colors and textures, and I've always had an eye for decor. I would still have to handle customers, but if my business plan proceeds as planned, I would be able to hire someone to take over some of the front desk duties and client interactions and bury myself in the back before long."

"You have a business plan? Then this is more than just a fantasy?"

She flushed at that and stood, almost looking like she might bolt. "No, it's just a dream for someday."

"A down the road kind of thing?" He said, letting his tone tell her he wasn't buying it at all.

She lifted a shoulder and let it fall. "Something like that."

"You've got four weeks off now. Why don't you take that time to do some more research. Maybe go look at space downtown? I assume you'd want to rent a storefront downtown?" James knew enough about her career and enough about the show jumping world to know that even without her family's money, she would probably have a nest egg to start her business with. Someone at her level of competition would be bringing in prize money that could support a start-up if it wasn't too costly.

Of course, a lot of people would have to put a lot of that money back into the horses they rode and competition fees and stuff. Her family probably paid for all that.

He watched as she crossed to Tess's stall and ran her hand over the horse's muzzle before turning to limp away from him.

"Can't. Even though I'm injured, I'm still attending most of the local shows."

There was something she wasn't saying there. He would guess it was an expectation. The demand that she be there. He remembered in sports in high school, even if you were hurt, you rode the bench. He supposed it was something along those lines. Still, he wondered, as she said goodbye and slipped out of the barn, how long she would continue to live for the people around her instead of living for herself.

CHAPTER EIGHT

James woke to the sensation of Lulu lying on him, paws on his shoulders. The weight grounded him, telling him instantly that the images in his mind were only those of a nightmare. He allowed himself a second to bury his head in her soft fur before reaching for the notebook next to his bed.

He scribbled notes, writing everything he could remember about the dream.

Boots that were too clean. Boots on dirt but no dirt on the boots.

Pallets and crates. The sight of boots on concrete floors. Gunshots.

He could hear the voice that had been haunting his dreams lately, but it never seemed to come through clearly enough for him to identify it. "What the fuck?"

The words rang over and over in James's mind. There was no accent. It was American.

Then an answering. "You fucked this up!" This one was a roar and it was a roar he recognized. The voice was Silva's.

Nothing else. The maddening blank space that filled the rest of the memory took over.

He reached, searching the shadows of the memory for something. A sound or smell. The smallest thing might be a hint. The smells of combat were so memorable, so vivid, surely that should stick out to him. But there was nothing.

He let his head fall back to the pillow, bringing one arm behind his head while the other arm moved to stroke Lulu. Closing his eyes and letting his mind wander back to the dream hadn't worked so far, but he tried it anyway.

Then he began to catalogue all the small things that had been eating at him since that initial nagging sensation that he needed to remember something.

It had started when he'd gone to the Pentagon to be debriefed. That wasn't the typical course of action for a soldier, but his situation had been different. He'd had information on the rebel groups and cartels working in that area. He'd talked mostly to desk colonels—the guys who didn't go into the field anymore.

He had met with General Brophy, one of the people responsible for pulling him out of there. He'd seen Colonel Gray when he'd first been brought to the USNS Comfort, the military hospital ship that had been his first stop after the rescue helo that pulled him out. He'd been really out of it then, though. Malnourished as all hell and not really in his right mind.

By then, his life was centered on the one thing he wanted. An opening. A chance to kill Silva. To avenge Catalina.

When the rescuers had come, they'd taken him out of there before he got close enough. He'd been too weak to find out if they had killed Silva when they got James out of there.

When he saw General Brophy at the Pentagon after a month of treatment in Walter Reed, the General had talked to him for hours about everything and nothing. Not a damned bit of the conversation had been about what had happened or what James had seen and done over there. It made a difference. Somehow, just that time, talking to a man who understood some of what he'd been through but didn't feel the need to talk about it had made a difference.

But when they got to the end of that time, James had asked if Silva was still alive. Brophy's answer was yes, as far as he knew. James didn't know how to deal with that. How to handle knowing the man who'd taken everything from him went on living and breathing.

It was during one of the long hours of debriefing that he'd had the first flash of memory. Not even memory, really. It was the ghost of a memory. Just a feeling that there was something he should know but didn't.

Part of him thought it could just be an idea the colonels had put in his head with all their questions. Colonel Gray was the one who'd dug at the memories the most, like someone determined to pick at a scab that wasn't ready to fall off yet. In the end, James had hated the man. He sat behind his desk and gave orders, not having the sense or recent enough field experience to understand the full implications of what he was telling his soldiers to do. Not like General Brophy, who not only had the field experience to back up his commands, but the kind of mind that remembered what it had been like on the ground. To see the implications of his work at a desk and understand the exact tie between that work to each and every man his commands affected.

James sat up and grabbed the notebook again as Lulu resettled herself a little further away from him. Once her job was done, she had no problem going back to sleep.

Pentagon, he wrote, followed by Gray, Simms, and

Coltrane, the names of the three colonels who had done the majority of the questioning. He put a star next to Gray, then put another one near Coltrane's name. He thought that maybe the first scrap of memory had happened when Coltrane was talking, and he felt like there was something familiar about Coltrane.

Maybe it was just the questions that made him want to remember now in a way he never had before. Or maybe it was the guilt that he was back at all. He was here and Catalina was not.

He closed his eyes against the onslaught of images. Soft eyes on his, smooth cool hands on his fevered skin. The smooth lilt of her voice as she talked to him. She'd saved him.

He looked down at his legs, still bearing the scars of that firefight. He could feel the heat licking up his skin.

Then she'd been there, and she'd made the pain bearable. She'd made it all bearable for a while. Until she hadn't. Until she was gone.

CHAPTER NINE

There was something about the early morning preparation for a horse show that Presley always loved. It started before the arrival at the show, when she'd come into the barn and flick on the lights to see horses popping their heads over the stalls. She'd stand on her step stool and braid manes and tails while the horses stood patiently on crossties. Everything would still be dark and quiet outside the barn and the sun would only start to come up after they'd led the horses into the trailer and pulled out onto the road.

They would pull into a show, forming rows in an open field and set up their area like a little campground of horse trailers. And then, she'd do what she was doing now. She would grab an egg and cheese sandwich on a roll wrapped in foil and a cup of coffee. It was a ritual that was soothing in its familiarity.

She stood now, with her coffee in hand and the wrapper from her sandwich wadded up in the pocket of her vest, watching at the side of one of the rings.

"I was sorry to hear you were sidelined."

Presley turned at the sound of Harry Trager's quiet voice. "Thank you. It's just for another few weeks, I hope."

He nodded, but his focus was now on the rider in the ring. "Steady, steady," he said under his breath, despite the fact the rider wasn't one of his. The teen on the horse wasn't at the level of riders that Harry worked with.

That was the way Harry Trager was. If he got the chance, he would pull the rider aside and offer a tip or two. Not in a way that said he was arrogant and knew it all. For Harry it was more about the love of what they all did. About the love of the ride, the love of the sport, the love of the way rider and horse could come together in an incredible way inside the ring.

As horse and rider left the ring and the next pair was announced, Harry turned his eyes to her again. "I heard Tess fell. Is she okay?"

"Yeah, she's fine. She spooked at a snake and then stumbled when she shied."

"You were lucky."

Presley didn't need to be told that. Although she had of course known riders whose horses had fallen on them with only a sore body to show for it, she'd also known many who'd broken bones or worse. She could remember one accident when she was younger when a rider ended up needing a knee reconstructed.

"I threw myself mostly clear of her." *And then a gorgeous knight in shining armor came to my rescue. Well, not armor. Jeans. Those jeans on James...*

Presley shook herself loose of the thoughts but couldn't stop the smile that came to her face.

Luckily for her, Harry Trager wouldn't notice the secretive nature of the smile or the fact she blushed. If he did notice, he wouldn't put two and two together and figure out it had anything to do with a man. Harry's observational skills were reserved for horses and riders, provided those riders were up on a horse, not crutches.

"Becky Layne is riding your Feldspar today?" He asked, his eyes going back to the ring. "She'll do well by him," Harry said, without waiting for her confirmation. He had turned back to the ring to watch as the next rider approached a jump. She could hear Harry's sigh as the rider tried to fit one too many strides in before the jump.

"She will. She's got a nice steady hand and he's been doing well with her in training." Presley thought for a minute that if she were to retire, Becky might take Feldspar into her string permanently.

She had to stop thinking that way. Her parents could talk of nothing but her getting back onto the circuit and she owed that much to them. People might not realize it, but her mom had sacrificed a lot to Presley's career. Sure, her mom had seemed to love every minute of it, but surely there had been times when her mom would have preferred not to travel so much, not to have to wake up with Presley before the sun was up to help her groom horses and braid manes.

When she was young, they'd only had the one horse per show to prep, but as she gained experience, she'd started bringing two to three horses per show. Her mom had been there to help her manage all that, not to mention simply managing the pressure that entering the Grand Prix level at a young age had brought. Presley had been two years younger than any of her closest competition. She hadn't been the type of girl to rebel, even in her teen years, but there had been days when she hadn't exactly made her mother's job easy, by any means. Days she'd been moody and snotty in the way only a teenager could.

Surely her mother hadn't wanted the job of organizing

tutors and keeping up with all the homeschooling requirements that let Presley compete at such high levels at such a
young age? When Presley had made it to the U.S. Olympic
team, her mother had gone with her, living months away
from her husband and her home so she could be with
Presley as the team prepped for their Olympic run. Her
mom had done that three times over the years and hadn't
complained a bit.

Someone came up to Harry on the other side and he
was lost in conversation with them. Presley wandered away
from the fence, heading back to the Royale Stables trailer to
check in on the horses. They'd brought four that day. Two
were horses that normally filled out her string and two were
horses her dad trained for other owners and their riders.

Becky sat on the wheel well of the trailer, pulling her
socks up. "Hey, Pres. Your dad is up in the back ring with
Porter."

Presley nodded and took a seat in one of the director's
chairs they'd set up outside the trailer. She lifted her ankle
up to rest on a cooler. "Is Porter feeling better?"

Porter Wylie was her father's new student and Presley
had a feeling he wouldn't last long, poor guy. His parents
wanted him to train with the great Lawrence Royale, but he
didn't have the temperament for it.

Her father was a hard man. While you couldn't actually
say he abused his charges, he had high expectations.
Anyone riding under him felt it to the core when they let
him down. He pushed hard in training and harder in the
ring. He never pulled punches and if he wasn't happy with
how you were doing something, you could plan to stay on
the horse's back until you could barely move before he'd
release you with instructions to be back first thing in the
morning.

Becky grimaced. "He threw up minutes before they headed up."

Presley sighed. "Maybe I can gently push his parents toward Harry."

Becky grinned. "Harry would be more his speed."

Harry was as hard as her father in some ways. He was exacting and held his students to a high standard, but if he wanted them to stay and work longer, he'd ask them how they felt they were doing. Then he'd ask what they thought they needed to do to make a change. He'd guide them to the solution of longer lessons and greater focus. He didn't berate or belittle the way her father could. The words that came from Harry's mouth never cut.

Presley's phone buzzed and she slipped it out of her pocket, looking at the screen.

The Cambury people are up at the main tent.

Her father didn't need to say any more. It was expected she would know that if the Cambury Veterinary Supply reps were in the main tent, Presley needed to get herself there, too. Cambury had been her main sponsors for years. Probably over a decade at this point. She needed to put in an appearance, woo them, and let them see she'd be back on top soon.

She stood, waving to Becky, who was now pulling on her boots. It was time to go earn her keep.

CHAPTER TEN

Presley pulled her truck slowly along the drive at Bishop Ranch. She didn't want to wake the house up, but she'd been on the road for almost a week, and she wanted to check on Tess before heading home.

Honestly, what she wanted was to bury her head in Tess's mane and wrap her arms around the large horse's neck. It had been a long week of talking and being "on" for other people. Her parents, her sponsors, the other riders. That much continuous "on" time—as she always thought of time when she had to constantly engage with other people—always wore Presley out. This was probably what she hated the most about being injured. When Presley was competing, she could disappear to her trailer and hide away in her changing room, telling anyone who asked that she was re-braiding her hair or taking a minute to focus before going up to the ring.

Anytime she'd been out with an injury, there wasn't that chance to find chunks of downtime throughout the day. People expected a competitor to want time to focus on getting into the right frame of mind before entering the ring.

When you weren't competing, it didn't work that way. Unless she told people she needed to rest her leg, but her mother would have had a coronary at that. Showing any kind of weakness that might put her return to greatness into jeopardy wouldn't have been acceptable.

She shut her truck door softly, then walked to the barn door, sliding it open with a soft call to Tess. Mostly she wanted to let the horses all know it was her entering the barn.

"Hey, Pres," came a soft voice in response and her heart kicked over at the sound of James's voice.

She walked farther into the aisle to find him at the other end of the barn, only the light of the tack room spilling out to illuminate the area.

"What are you doing here?" It was obvious what he was doing at that very moment. He was giving Cade's horse, Cayenne, an ear rub that had the horse looking like he might melt into a puddle right there. Lulu stood silently by his side. His sentry.

Presley thought about what it would be like to have those hands on her. She bet she would look a lot like that, too. All puddle-headed and ready to melt.

"Couldn't sleep," he said simply. "You just get back? Cade said you were in the northeast this week at shows."

"Mm-hm," she murmured, going to Tess.

James moved over to stand next to her and she felt the heat of him even though there were a good several inches of space between them.

She reached to put her hands on either side of Tess's face when the horse pushed her muzzle into Presley's chest. "I just wanted to say hi to her."

He was looking at where Tess pressed her face to Presley's chest and she felt her cheeks heat, for some reason.

He cleared his throat and reached a hand up to Tess's ear, giving her the same treatment he'd just given Cayenne. "She's been great this week. We've been out just about every day."

Presley grinned as Tess moved closer and closer to James. "Clearly, her loyalties are shifting."

He laughed. "Nah, she'll always be your girl." He looked to the horse. "Won't you, baby?"

And now Presley was jealous of Tess. First Cayenne, now Tess. This was bad.

"I think the riding has been really good for my legs," he said.

"Oh?" Presley wasn't surprised that riding would help him with his injuries. It was great therapy. She hadn't known exactly what his injuries entailed, though.

"Yeah. I get a lot of pain in my legs. They were burned."

"You don't limp," she said, then wanted to kick herself. She had no idea why she'd said it.

"Not usually, no, but I get shooting pains in them sometimes."

"But the riding helps?" She figured she would bring it back around to his initial statement since she had no idea what to say.

"It does. I don't know, I guess maybe just using them more is helping."

"I think they say there's something about the way the rocking movement of the horse moves you. It helps with gait. And I've always thought there was something to the heat of the horse's body against your muscles, you know?"

She looked to him and found him watching her with an intensity that both caught her off guard and stole her breath.

She looked away.

"How was your trip?" He asked.

She thought for a minute, not really wanting to give him the pat answer that everything was great. For some reason, she didn't like the idea of giving him the expected answer that did nothing to say how she really felt.

"It was long." She stopped herself from explaining that she didn't like being on for the crowds and people who wanted face time with her or her father.

"But you'd rather be arranging flowers?" He asked, a teasing tone lightening his voice.

"Something like that." Actually, the idea of sitting and working on an arrangement was exactly what she'd like to do. It was calming to look at a piece, move something here, take away something there, add just the right splash of color or find the right weight or texture of flower.

"Will you get very far behind with missing so many shows?"

"In the year-end rankings, you mean?"

"Is that what it's about? The rankings?"

She nodded. "Sort of. For this year, for me, yes. It's not an Olympic year." She'd been to the Olympics the previous year, bringing home an individual Silver and a team Gold. "But there's qualification for the World Equestrian Games, if I don't drop far enough to be out of the running."

"You went to the Olympics?"

Presley grinned. She was damned proud of her Olympic medals and the time she'd spent with her team held some of her favorite memories. "Three times."

He whistled. "Damn, girl. I guess I should have guessed as much with the way you fly over those jumps. Will you drop behind too much to make the World Games because of your injury?" He seemed to move closer and Presley found it hard to control her thoughts with him that close to her.

"I, uh, it depends on how my competitors all fare while

I'm out. I might be able to make up some lost ground when I get back. If I'm not out too long and if the top riders don't all run away with the rankings while I'm out."

They might not. Petra Albescu had performed exceptionally poorly over the weekend and Donna Mooreland, one of Harry's riders, had struggled in the jump-off against a rider who really wasn't as good as she was. That was the way riding was. Sometimes, even if your competition wasn't as good as you, your mount had a poor day or you just weren't on target the way you needed to be. A lot of factors needed to come together in the ring for things to go your way in the ribbons.

She looked back toward James, finding his gaze on her again and she would swear he'd moved closer, making her heart slop around in her chest. She didn't know what to say, so she just stared.

Presley searched her mind for something to say, but found a giant blank. Her eyes flew to his and, she realized, he didn't seem to be waiting for her to say anything. His eyes were on her mouth and the air was thick with a tension she recognized but didn't have a whole lot of experience with. She might have made a sound, part moan, part question.

He answered by bringing his mouth to hers, not moving his body at all. He simply lowered his head and touched his lips to hers. The moment was perfect, and still, and all she wanted but hadn't known she wanted. And then, in a heartbeat, it changed.

The moment seemed to burst to flame and his whole body moved then, turning to take hold of her. He drew her in, pulling her to him. Pressing their bodies together as Presley's head spun.

His mouth was seeking, demanding, needing, and she found answering need spiraled through her.

Now she moaned again, fully this time without question, without hesitation.

His response was a growl as he moved his mouth to her neck and she felt the kiss rocket through her body. She felt it through her stomach and lower, then down through her toes which seemed to curl in a way that made her truly appreciate the saying *toe-curling kiss*.

Presley didn't know when her hands had flown to his shoulders, but she clung to him, wanting to be closer. She ran her hands over his shoulders, then up his neck, to his short-cropped hair. She splayed her fingers over him, a pool of desire taking over.

And then he stopped. So quickly she thought she might fall over when he stepped away.

His eyes were wide. Even in the dim light she could see the horror in his eyes at what had happened and immediately, she wished she could sink into the blackness that covered the farthest corners of the barn.

At least he didn't apologize. That would have made things worse.

Instead, he turned without a word and walked away, his body stiff with regret.

CHAPTER ELEVEN

James liked the way he could sometimes seem to make time stand still when he worked with wood. Or maybe it was that he could make time move so quickly, he didn't realize it was going by. Whatever it was, it let him escape his thoughts for a while. Today, he'd left the barn doors open wide but had the lights off inside the barn.

He was sanding again, the repetition of the action clearing his mind. He guessed for most people, hand sanding would lead to boredom. He liked the simplicity of it. He needed to find the emptiness that would let his mind give up on reliving the kiss with Presley over and over again.

He moved one hand over the wood with the sanding paper in hand, then followed it with a stroke of the other hand, feeling the grain of the wood. Sanding hand, free hand. Sanding hand, free hand. The pattern wasn't the most efficient for achieving a smooth surface, but he'd found it was the best for clearing his mind.

One minute, James was sanding, and the next, he looked up and saw the silhouette of a man in uniform standing in the doorway of the barn. The flashback hit hard as he spiraled back to another building and another time.

His squad mate, Jordy Peters, screaming at James to get back. The faces of Brian Russell and Matt McPherson as they turned to run, shouting at him.

Then Lulu was there, pulling him out of it.

James shook as he dug his hands in her hair. Somehow, he'd landed on his ass on the barn floor, Lulu in his lap and the calm eyes of General Brophy watching him.

The General sat on his haunches a few feet away, waiting as James huddled with Lu.

When a few minutes had passed, the General stood and offered James his hand, lifting him to his feet when James took it.

"Are they happening often?" He asked with the strong but quiet voice James had come to expect from him.

"Not too often." He lied to the man, but could tell the General wasn't buying it. "What are you doing here?"

If the General thought it was rude to ask the question, he didn't let on. "Visiting Phoebe. She and Shane have been wanting to take a trip to DC, but I like the pie at the diner here."

James let out a laugh as he remembered Laura telling him the General spent a lot of time with one of the sisters who owned the local diner.

The General shrugged. "Gina makes good pie."

James shook his head. He made a mental note of all he'd just seen in the flashback. He'd need to write it in his journal when the General left. He sat in one of the chairs at the table while the General went to the other. He knew better than to tease Brophy for his crush on the diner owner. The General might act like his friend more than his superior, but there was a line you didn't cross.

General Brophy took a piece of paper from his pocket and slid it across the table to James. "It's the name of a counselor that works with veterans nearby. I don't know her personally, but she's a veteran herself and she comes highly recommended from people I trust."

James looked at the paper but didn't take it. He'd seen a shrink when he was in the hospital after they'd pulled him out. It helped, but only so much.

Brophy leaned forward. "They took four years from you, Soldier. You can't get those four years back, but you can make sure they don't take anymore from you."

Their eyes caught and held, and James reached out to take the paper. He shook just thinking of the idea of driving to a counselor, of telling someone what he was thinking. Then again, the flash he'd just had of the firefight in South America was the most detailed he'd had yet. Maybe talking to someone would help him remember. He looked down at the name.

Sarah Garrett.

He looked at the General. "You could have brought me pie, too."

That got him a laugh. "Next time."

James wondered if maybe he'd be able to go to the diner himself by the next time the General visited. An image of Presley and the kiss in the barn ran across his mind and he knew there were other things worth pushing for. Maybe it was time for him to push himself. He just didn't know if he could ever get himself to the point where he'd feel worthy of Presley Royale. Where he'd feel like he wouldn't just be saddling her with a man who could only bring her down. Because, really, what did he have to offer anyone right now?

Not a damned thing.

CHAPTER TWELVE

Three days and James still hadn't been able to clear Presley Royale from his senses. He sat cross legged on the floor of his loft, eyes closed, meditating.

Four years in the hands of madmen and he'd meditated through hunger, pain, and sickness. But one kiss from Presley had gotten so deep under his skin, he couldn't clear his mind.

He could still smell her, taste her, feel the soft curve of her body as he pressed her against him. He opened his eyes and looked down at his hands where Lulu had begun to lick.

As a PTSD support dog, she was trained to interrupt any behaviors associated with agitation or anxiety, so when he'd started flexing his hands into fists, she'd come forward to stop the behavior. Little did she know he was only trying to rid his hands of the sensation of touching Presley.

He rewarded Lulu with a scratch behind the ears, then closed his eyes to start again.

He'd begun meditating again to see if he could draw out the memories trapped in his mind. The nightmares had continued, as confusing and out-of-reach as they'd ever been and with Lulu trained to wake him any time they began, he wasn't going to get more information that way.

He needed to get the memories to come when he was awake.

They wouldn't come, though. All that came when he closed his eyes were images of Presley. Only this time, they mingled with memories of Catalina. One minute, he was holding Catalina, making love to her, then she switched with Presley and Presley took over. Neither woman let him get to the memories that really mattered, the memories of what happened that night.

James cursed and stood, giving up.

He crossed to the window and looked down at the barn. It had rained the day before, so he hadn't been riding. He should take Tess out and exercise her.

He almost missed his phone ringing. It sat buried under a pile of laundry on his bedside table. He rescued it and saw the number for the shrink the General had given him.

"Hello," he said, part of him wanting to hang up the phone so he didn't have to deal with reality.

"Hey, is this James?"

He stopped for a second, wondering if he was wrong. He'd thought it was the therapist's number, but she didn't sound at all like he'd thought she might.

When he didn't answer, she went on. "James? That you or did I dial wrong?" He could hear the shuffling of papers. "I'm horrible with details. Hell, I might have dialed my ob-gyn's office for all I know."

James broke out in a grin. He knew this woman. Not personally, of course. He'd never met Sarah Garrett, but he recognized her. She was the kind of tough woman who could go toe-to-toe with the guys when they were overseas.

He cleared his throat. "Yeah, this is James."

She acted like she hadn't just faked him out and gotten him to talk. She also acted like they'd already gone through the preliminary niceties of a conversation, and jumped right in. "Listen, I'm gonna tell you, the best way for you to get yourself in here to talk to me is if we make an appointment soon, so you have less time to get your panties in a bunch over it. I also think you should make that appointment for early in the morning when there are very few people out and about. Easier on you to get here if you don't have to drive in traffic and you won't have to see anyone but me. My receptionist doesn't even come in until eight, so if you bring your ass in at a God-awful hour—say, six o'clock—you're not going to run into her."

Apparently, the doc had this shit figured out.

Her next words told him she thought following her advice was a given. "Tomorrow at six?"

There was only the slightest hesitation on his part. He'd have to see if Laura could drive him. She was usually up early, so it wouldn't be a problem. "Yeah," he said before he could chicken out. "See you then."

He let out a breath, and grabbed a shirt from the back of the chair where he recycled most of his clothes until they were ready to be washed. Time to get Tess out and go for a ride. The more he could keep his mind off the appointment he'd just made, the better off he'd be.

When he'd groomed and saddled Tess, he walked out the large double doors at the end of the barn with her, planning to go to the mounting block near the side pasture. His sister Laura called out to him before he got there.

She was waving at him from ten yards away. James headed toward her instead of the mounting block.

"Hey, Rabbit," he said, using the nickname he'd used

with her as a child. She'd been like a little scared bunny when she was younger. Not at all like the woman who stood before him.

The name gutted him, reminding him of all the ways he'd let her down.

She seemed to brighten at it, though, eyes sparkling as she glared at him in mock annoyance. "You getting ready to ride?"

He didn't answer her. Just looked over at the horse with her saddle and bridle on and back to Laura, who laughed as though she'd realized how stupid the question was.

James moved to a fallen log in the grass and used it to mount Tess, then put a hand down to Laura. "Come with me?"

She looked up at him for a minute, and he knew she was getting ready to argue. He quirked a brow in the way he had when they were younger and he'd wanted to dare her into doing something he knew would take pushing.

She shook her head, but reached an arm up as he moved his leg forward, letting her use the stirrup to climb behind him on Tess. She wrapped her arms around him and he grinned as he moved Tess into a walk, heading for the ring.

"I need to ask you for a favor." Somehow asking her when she wasn't facing him seemed easier. Not that asking his sister to help him was hard. It was admitting he was going to a shrink that was, though he didn't know why that should be. Hell, people probably expected him to be off his rocker.

"Anything."

He knew she meant it. "I have an appointment tomorrow morning and I need a ride. It's early, though. I have to be there at six and it's twenty minutes away." He'd looked and Sara's office was in the next town over.

"No problem. As long as I swing through and pick up donuts for Jamie on the ride home, she'll be happy to help Cade muck out stalls while I take you to your appointment."

"Thanks." He should spend more time with his niece, Jamie. Maybe he could have donuts with her after his appointment.

"You like riding Tess for Presley, don't you?"

"Mm-hm."

"And you like Presley," she went on.

He didn't respond. She knew this already. She'd warned him that Presley was too complicated for him and that he was too complicated for Presley. He understood that. Hell, no one knew better than he that Presley was better off without him.

He went past the ring to the large field Cade kept trimmed and clear of rocks and let Tess move at a lazy pace around the perimeter. Most of the time, the horse was pushing for a faster pace, but today, she seemed content to stroll while he and Laura talked.

"I think maybe I was wrong," Laura said quietly, to his back. He stiffened.

"About what?"

"About Pres. I think maybe you'd be good for each other."

James wanted to shake her and ask what the hell had given her that idea, but he recognized the overreaction and clamped down on it.

"I don't think she needs me messing with her life." He hadn't clamped down on his emotions hard enough if the rigid edge to his tone was any indication.

"Why do you say that?" Laura had a way of softening her questions.

Still, he didn't have an answer for her. Didn't she understand he was poison to everyone around him? Damn it, she'd been on the receiving end of his poison. Why couldn't she see that he was bad for her? Bad for Presley?

Not for the first time, he knew he'd been selfish in taking Laura up on coming to the ranch when he got out of the hospital. He hadn't had any place else to go and coming here meant he hadn't been forced to think about where to go or what to do. It had been the easy way out.

And it had been wrong. He needed to get out of here. To put some space between himself and the people who loved him. The people he loved. They'd all just get dragged into the shit pile in his head if he didn't watch it. They'd start to hope he might someday be normal, and that wasn't possible.

"Hey, talk to me. Tell me what you're thinking in that overtaxed brain of yours."

"Overtaxed, huh?" He asked.

"Yeah, overtaxed. Why do you think you shouldn't be involved with Presley?"

"I'm just not, it's not, I . . ." He didn't know how to say it. "I don't want to hurt her the way I've hurt everyone else. I've got so much shit happening in my head right now, I can barely function. There's no way I won't drag her down with me if I let myself get close. I can't do that to her. It's bad enough after years of letting you down, I'm living off of you and Cade now."

"What the hell are you talking about?" Laura leaned to one side, as though she could come around to see his face, despite the fact that they were on top of a horse. "What does that mean? You've never let me down."

James's laugh was bitter. "I left you in a hellish marriage for three years. If that's not failure, I don't know what is."

"Stop this horse," she said, taking him by surprise. She hit his back with a small fist for good measure.

"Laura—" She didn't let him finish. She pounded her fists on his back in a way only a little sister can do.

James slowed Tess to a stop and gave Laura his arm to help her slide to the ground.

"Get down here." She had both hands on her hips, letting him know she meant business. Not that he couldn't ride away, but he wouldn't do that to her.

He slid from the saddle, then spent a few minutes focused on Tess, slipping the bit from her mouth but leaving the bridle in place so the horse could tear at the grass under a nearby tree.

When he turned back to Laura, her eyes flashed. "You have never once in your life let me down, James Lawless. You've been there from the day I was born when no one else was."

She didn't have to name the no-one-elses in that statement. Their mother had died when Laura was too young to remember her and their father had been emotionally abusive and cruel. It had been the two of them against the world growing up.

But then Laura had met Patrick Kensington, a man who came from money and power. The Kensingtons were a powerful family, with several senators in the lineage and the kind of money that would never run low, even if the family did nothing to grow their coffers. James hadn't seen through Patrick Kensington's charade. Hadn't seen him for the monster he truly was. James had signed up for the Army and taken off, moving from basic into a specialized program that had him in black ops training before he knew it. There were few chances for him to call home and visiting wasn't an option most of the time.

Still, the few times James had called her, he'd been put off by her husband, always with an excuse about why Laura couldn't call. He'd emailed with her only to find out years later, it had been her husband emailing all that time. James hadn't seen through any of it. Hadn't realized how controlling her husband was. Hadn't seen that she was in trouble. And Laura had paid the price, because she was living in a home where terror reigned and her husband treated her worse than their father ever could have. Her husband's brand of abuse had been physical instead of just emotional. He'd raped and beaten her on a regular basis.

James didn't say any of that. "Didn't I?"

She shook her head, moving now to reach up and put her hands on his shoulders, despite the difference in their height. "No, you didn't. It wasn't on you. What happened with Patrick was not on you, do you hear me, James?" She said each word slowly, clearly as though dealing with her three-year-old. "And I wouldn't trade any of it."

James stepped back, letting her hands fall. "What? How the hell can you say that?"

She smiled at him, a small smile that tipped the corners of her mouth back, but it was a sad gesture. "How could I want to change it? My journey isn't one that I would have chosen. And yes, I have regrets. But it was the journey that brought me to Cade. It gave me my daughter. It's the journey that brought me to a place where I've known more joy, more kindness, more love than I ever could have hoped."

James couldn't breathe, but Laura went on, oblivious to the turmoil roiling inside him.

"But more importantly, James, it was my journey to take and it's my journey to own. You can't have it. You can't have the responsibility for it. You can't have the burden of it. I won't let you."

James could only stare at Laura. She was so damned strong. So much stronger than the girl he'd left years before after her wedding day.

There was only one problem, though. She could absolve him of his sins against her. She could tell him he couldn't own the failures where she was concerned.

But she didn't know the half of it. She didn't know how fucked up things were inside his head. She couldn't know that he would only drag Presley down if he let her get close. He wanted so badly to cling to all of them and let the people and the ranch take on some of his burden, but what would happen if instead of fixing him, it spread this dark poison that was in him to all of them? What if he did nothing more than drag them all down with him?

CHAPTER THIRTEEN

Even with all the people and horses surrounding her at one of the region's biggest horse shows, Presley didn't think she would be able to get the feel of James's kiss out of her head. It had been days and still, she relived the moment again and again. She tried to force her mind to go to the look on his face when he'd realized what they were doing and, she guessed, who he was doing it with. Regret didn't begin to cover the emotions he'd been feeling. The emotions that had been evident in his expression.

Instead, nothing but the kiss, the feel of his hands on her, the feel of his mouth as he'd moved to her neck, seemed to consume her thoughts. She couldn't get the images to stop.

Their horses had been brought to the grounds twenty-four hours in advance, as required at all United States Equestrian Foundation competitions at the Grand Prix level. Presley had arrived the day before and was expected to be ringside any minute to watch her competition, but she found herself holding back, waiting in the barn to try to catch a few more minutes of solitude.

She let herself into the tack room. In a few minutes, the barn would be alive again with people, but for now it was blissfully quiet, the scent of leather and straw and horses a soothing balm.

Presley could see out into the barn aisle through the open door of the room, but she knew from her position at the back of the small space that she wouldn't be visible to anyone unless they looked directly in. If someone came into the tack room, she'd say she dropped a hair band and was looking for it.

The sound of a whinny came to her from down the aisle. There was nothing out of place about the sound. Until it changed. There was a loud bang that was unmistakable, the sound of a horse's foot hitting the side of the stall, then the sound came again and again.

Presley shot from the room, seeing a flash of dark color coming from down at the end of the barn. But her eyes went to a stall a few doors over.

When she reached the stall and looked over it, she shouted for help, then slipped in. The horse lay on his side, seizing as stiff legs hit the side of the small space again and again. She thought it was one of Harry's horses. Davenport. She'd seen him a few times at previous shows.

Presley knew she was taking a risk. A seizing horse was dangerous, pure and simple. Still, she let herself in the door and went to the horse's head, pressing her weight on it to hold it in place.

She was joined by others, one of whom was the veterinarian. Within minutes the seizing was under control and the horse lay breathing in great gusts and snorts, sweat slicking his body.

"What happened?" The vet asked her, a little accusation lacing the words.

"I don't know." Presley took a breath and nodded at the aisle. "I was in the tack room when I heard him kicking."

The owner of the horse came down the aisle then and there were several questions fired back and forth from the owner and the vet. Within minutes, there was someone from the show organizers present. At the end of it, when it became clear the horse had no history of seizures and nothing in his recent medical history to suggest he would have one now, blood was drawn to see if the horse had been dosed with something.

Presley couldn't tell if the veterinarian was blaming her or the owner when he said, "My guess is someone tried to inject something into a vein and hit the carotid artery instead. The seizure would have been immediate."

Presley thought of the flash she'd seen when she came out of the tack room. Had it been a person exiting? She thought so, but she wasn't sure. She bit her lip. "I think maybe someone was leaving when I came out of the tack room. I saw someone. But it was only out of the corner of my eye. It might have been someone just walking past the doors."

Harry came in, but his attention went right to the horse and stayed with it. The horse's owner and several show officials then spent over twenty minutes questioning her before they seemed to understand she didn't have any more information to offer them. She simply hadn't seen or heard anything that could help.

"Presley!" It was her mother's voice behind her and the anger in it told Presley her mother was going to make a scene. Fantastic. Someone had let her mother know she was all but being accused of drugging a horse. "What's going on here?"

The show officials had the sense to look a little embarrassed. One of them rushed to assure her mother they were just talking to her in the hopes she would remember something that could help them.

The vet had taken blood samples to see what had been given to the horse. He found swelling at the site of the injection but finding out what had been pushed into the artery might give them a clue as to who was behind it.

If it was a drug designed to steady the horse, to calm him before going into the arena, that would suggest the owner might be behind it. As it was, the owner was looking more than nervous now that Presley's mother had shown up. In all likelihood, they were probably hoping her father didn't arrive on the scene.

If the drug was one to pump the horse up, it could have been a competitor hoping to throw the horse off, make him have a bad ride. The horse was pacing at the moment, but that could be the result of the stress of having had the seizure. He might crash any minute.

Presley and her mother left the area, leaving the mess for the show officials and vet to sort out. She'd told them all she could, and frankly, she was ready to go home for the day. This show wasn't so far away from Evers that they needed to stay overnight.

"What were you doing in there?" Her mother hissed as they walked away, a smile plastered on her face in case anyone was watching. They were watching, of course. News had spread about the incident to at least everyone in the vicinity of the barn.

I was hiding from everyone.

That answer probably wouldn't do. "I was looking for something I thought I left in the tack room."

Her mother raised a brow. "On a day when you aren't even riding?"

"I was in there earlier talking to Becky. I dropped a hair tie."

"You dropped a hair tie and thought you'd, what? Pick it up off the ground and put it back in your hair?"

Presley didn't answer. She didn't know what her mother thought she was doing in the room. "Are you and Dad finished for the day? I thought Becky was the last to ride."

"She was, but your dad is waiting to watch a prospective student ride."

"Who's that?"

"Sandy Barrow might be looking for a new coach."

"Really?" Presley was surprised her father would consider taking her on. Sandy was notorious for her tantrums and for switching trainers as often as she switched out her shirt during a show. Which was a lot. "What on earth would make him consider..." She didn't finish the question. It had never been her place to question what her dad did, and it wasn't any more now than it had ever been.

Her mother gave her a hard look as they moved through people and horses, working their way to the long trailer that had hauled their horses and those of her father's students to the show.

Right, Presley thought. She had forgotten. You don't argue with the great Lawrence Royale, even if he wasn't around to hear it.

She shook her head. If her father wanted to take on a student who would give him nothing but grief, why should she try to talk him out of it? It wasn't any of her business.

She took a deep breath. "I'm going to sit in the truck for a bit. My ankle is aching. I want to put it up."

It wasn't a lie. She'd moved much too quickly on it when she'd seen the seizing horse thrashing on the ground.

"Did you reinjure yourself?" There was accusation in the tone.

"It's nothing, mom. I'm just tired. It hurts more after I've been on it a while."

She limped away, climbing up into the Suburban they'd followed the trailer in, leaning against one door and stretching her leg across the seat. She must have fallen asleep that way, because she woke some time later with a stiff neck and her father tapping on the window.

"Wake up, Pres. We're leaving."

Presley winced as she sat, putting her hand to the tight heat that flashed in her neck. She hit the button to unlock the car.

It became clear right away that her parents were fighting as they slid into the front seats.

"Where's Becky?" Becky had ridden to the show with them that morning and Presley assumed she'd be riding back with them.

"She's riding back in the truck." Her father's words were stiff. Enough so that she paused in buckling her seatbelt.

He was really angry.

Her father backed out of their spot in the grass field that had served as parking for the trailers and turned them toward the road. It was slow going, having to stop routinely as horses were led through the vehicles on the way back to their trailers.

Presley was thrown back to childhood. Her parents didn't fight more than other parents did, she thought. But whenever they did fight, Presley had always felt like it was somehow her fault. She would try to figure out what she had done and what she could do to fix it.

As the silence in the car dragged on, she ran through the

day. "Is this about Davenport's seizure? I wasn't hurt. And I was only trying to help."

Her mother sighed. "Leave it alone, Presley."

The sneer that crossed her father's face startled Presley. He could be cold and calculating, he could freeze you out when he wanted to, but the kind of scorn she'd seen in his eyes just then wasn't something she was used to seeing in him.

Unease crept over Presley. "I don't think I want to leave it alone."

If her parents thought anything of the fact she hadn't listened, they didn't say anything. In fact, they seem to be in their own world right now. There was something unspoken between them, and it was large and looming and more than a little terrifying to Presley. She was thirty years old, but she suddenly felt like a child again.

She could drop it, let them ride in silence for the rest of the two-hour drive back, but she didn't want to. She didn't want this feeling and she didn't want to let them make her feel like a child.

"Tell me what's going on." She didn't add a please. "Now."

Her father opened his mouth to speak, but to Presley's surprise, her mother cut him off.

"Lawrence!"

Her father shot her mother look. "What? You don't think she has the right to know?"

Her mother didn't answer, only turning to look out the window.

Silence reigned for several more minutes before her father spoke. "Your mother decided she would see to it that your standing wasn't affected in any great way while you were sidelined."

Unease had spun into dread as Presley looked from her mother to her father and back again. "Oh no, Mom, you didn't. Davenport? What did you do?"

Her mother was silent, not even turning her head.

"Dad?"

Her dad didn't answer. Neither of them spoke the rest of the ride home, leaving Presley to think about what she knew without being flat out told. Her mother was responsible for whatever drug had been pushed into Davenport.

Presley's mind spun. If it had been a Fédération Equestre Internationale event instead of a USEF one, the security at the stables and tents would have been much stricter. FEI events required badges to get through security.

No matter the security or lack thereof, Presley was intelligent enough to know that her mother wouldn't have done it herself. It wasn't her mother she saw leaving the stable that afternoon. She'd have hired somebody. Likely one of the grooms at the stable or one of the hired hands behind the scenes who was paid by the hour to take on the extra workload of running the show.

But the fact remained, her mother had thought so little about the health of that horse, about the safety of its rider, she was willing to do something unforgivable in Presley's eyes. Sure, there was a lot of drugging going on in the world of stadium jumping. It was an issue that the organizations with oversight were working to address.

It was also an issue her own father had strong feelings about. He might be hard as hell on his students, he might push them further than a lot of coaches would push, but he never allowed cheating. And he certainly never would have cheated in a way that put the horse at risk.

Presley's head spun for what seemed like an eternity, but was only the remaining hour-and-a-half of the drive back to their land. She would have thought they'd be eager to escape the confines of the car, ready to get away from one another. Instead, when her father cut the engine outside the barn, they sat in silence.

How would Presley go back and face the people her mother had tried to cheat? How could she face Harry and not tell him her mother had been the one behind the horse's seizure? How could she believe her mother wouldn't do it again? Hadn't done it before?

It was Presley who finally broke the silence when she realized the answer to all her questions was that she couldn't. She couldn't do this anymore. "I think I'm finished." She shook her head and sat up straighter. "No, I don't mean, I *think*." As the words came, she felt more strength come with them. She felt the determination of one who knows when it's truly time to act.

"I *am* finished. I'm retiring."

CHAPTER FOURTEEN

The ensuing argument with her parents was exhausting. Not that Presley would have expected anything less.

She honestly didn't know whether to feel surprise or pride in the fact that she hadn't given in, that she'd stuck with her decision to retire.

Now, driving toward Bishop Ranch, she began to feel an almost numb sort of panic take over. Walking away from all she knew, all she'd achieved over the years, was thrilling on one level and terrifying on another. But the knowledge that her mom would go to such extremes to keep Presley on top during her injury had sickened her. It also reminded her that her parents did a lot of what they did for themselves, not for her. Not for her career and not for what she wanted. For what they wanted. For what they could get out of her career.

She hadn't said that to them, and probably never would. She loved them and knew, in their own way, they loved her as well. Or at least she would continue to believe that. She had to.

She thought she was driving to the ranch to see Tess.

When she arrived, it instantly became obvious to her that she'd been driving toward James. She didn't stop at the animal barn, instead driving straight out to his barn. When she knocked on the door to the staircase that led to his loft she felt nothing close to confident. The last time she'd seen him he'd kissed the hell out of her and then all but ran out of the room.

When he opened the door, she found herself unable to put into words what she needed. She didn't seem able to say, "hold me," "kiss me," "make me feel better about everything."

He looked at her for a long minute before pushing the door wider and reaching out to take her hand. The feel of his strength, the warmth of his hand, washed over her.

When they got to the loft, he turned to her and opened his mouth and she knew there would be questions coming. What had happened? What was wrong? Or maybe not. Maybe he was opening his mouth to apologize for kissing her.

And she didn't want any of that. She brought her arms up around his neck and pulled him down to her, pulling his mouth to hers.

She felt the moment when he gave in and took control, making the kiss his own. The feeling was heady and intoxicating. Knowing she could entice him to the point of giving in. Feeling that control of his crashing to a halt. She'd seen his control, seen how hard he fought to keep everything under wraps. And right now, nothing about the man was under wraps.

His arms came up, his hands tangling in her hair as he tilted her head. The access he sought was freely given, and he growled as he turned his attention to her neck. Every part of her body tingled and burned with arousal, giving her the distraction she'd sought. Making her feel something other than the shock of realizing what her mother had done. Giving her the ability to ignore, for the moment, that she was about to throw away everything her life had been about up to that point. That she was about to walk out on a limb that was frightening and possibly very lonely.

She moaned as his kisses crossed to the nape of her neck and all but wept his name when his hands found her breasts.

He touched her over her shirt but quickly broke apart from her with a curse, only to lift her shirt and pull it over her head. He came back to her then and his hands and mouth were everywhere all at once. The feel of him on her like this left her wanting one thing—her hands on him. She tugged at his shirt and he stepped back to let her remove it, revealing hard muscle and smooth skin broken in many places by scars that told the story of his life.

It was a story that she knew he would probably never tell. Not to her, and probably not to anyone. Right now, that didn't matter. What mattered was her hands on him and his hands on her. She ran her fingers over the warm skin, reveling in the feel of him. Reveling in the way her own body responded to being able to touch him.

She had never experienced that before. A man's touch had always aroused her but there had never been something so exciting and thrilling about being able to put her hands on a man's body. And when he growled or moaned at something she did, the response was almost like a drug.

He walked them backward to his bed and sat on the edge, pulling her between his legs, spread wide to make room for her. He remained clothed from the waist down, but he quickly stripped her bare. He leaned in, tasting her breasts, her stomach, then lifting her and twisting until she lay on the bed and he knelt between her legs.

Each of them seemed lost in the swirl of arousal, her murmuring nonsense words as he used his tongue and hands to bring her to an earth-shattering orgasm.

She didn't hear the words he spoke, knowing only from their tone that they were words of appreciation and possibly even wonder.

JAMES KNEW he should stop this. His brain screamed at him to put an end to this, to send Presley away. He was past the point of reasoning, though. He had only enough control to go to his duffel and grab a condom. He bought a box of them when he left the hospital, then he'd gone to a seedy dive bar and picked up a woman whose smile had told him she would gladly spend the night with him and not expect anything in the morning.

He ignored the fact that, with that woman, the release had been nothing but pure physical bliss. The need to rid himself of the tension that had built inside him in the years since Catalina had died. With that woman, he'd closed his eyes and done his best to ignore the fact that she wasn't Catalina.

With Presley, he closed his eyes as well, but it had nothing to do with any memories of Catalina invading. Catalina was far from his mind, for the moment.

He closed his eyes now, because he couldn't bear to look at the woman he knew he would hurt in the morning. When she expected more from him, when she expected this to go somewhere.

He knew he was lowering himself beyond the dirt on her boots. That he owed her more respect than to use her body this way, but when she'd shown up on his doorstep he hadn't been able to say no to her.

There had been a look of such pain in her eyes it made his chest ache and he needed to reach out and pull her in.

And when she'd reached for him and kissed him like she needed him—not just anyone—but him... well, that had done him in.

He kissed his way back up her body, listening to the panting need in her breath. He should stop, talk to her, tell her. Make sure she knew damned well what this was, and more exactly, what it wasn't.

But he didn't. When she moaned and writhed beneath him, lifting her hips in a gesture that told him exactly what she wanted, he gave it to her. He sheathed himself in her slick heat, stopping once he was buried to the hilt.

He had to stop and catch his breath, but he kept his face buried in her neck, licking and nipping, but most importantly not looking at her.

She pressed her hips into him. "More, James, please."

With that, she set him loose and he moved within her, lost to the heat and the feel of her wrapped around him. He would hate himself when this was over, but for now he reveled in her. Only her.

CHAPTER FIFTEEN

Presley waited for James's breath to even out before sliding out from beneath his arm. It was the second time she had attempted the move. The first time, he'd caught her around the waist, pulling her into him and within minutes he ramped up the arousal again, entering her as soon as she was ready for him.

He'd taken her again as they lay spooned together, her back to his chest. The position had meant he was holding her wrapped in his arms and the feel of it had taken her breath away. More than that, it had meant that he wasn't able to bury himself as deeply within her, instead only rocking within her, in a teasing way that drove her mad with want and need.

She had struggled to turn around in his arms so that she could wrap her legs around him and let him plant himself deeper within her. But he hadn't let her, an almost rough laugh telling her he knew exactly what she wanted, but he wouldn't give it to her.

Instead he'd reached around and found her clitoris with one hand, driving her mad as their hips moved in tandem.

When they orgasmed again he'd slipped out of her and fallen back to sleep.

This time, he let her slip from the bed and she dressed quickly before stealing out of the room as Lulu watched from a bed in the corner.

She left because she didn't want to face the talk in the morning that would surely come. The conversation where he would tell her that there couldn't be anything between them. That what had happened was a mistake and something that couldn't happen again.

She knew if she stayed there and faced him in the morning she wouldn't be able to put on the false bravado that would let her say she understood it could only be physical. She needed time to get herself under control before she could play that game. Presley wasn't like that. She wasn't the kind of woman who could sleep with someone and have it be purely physical without letting her emotions get involved.

She knew she needed time to be able to mask the feelings that James was slowly bringing out in her. She would face him after she'd gotten herself together enough to play the part.

It was nearly four in the morning when Presley slipped into her own bed, finally allowing herself to close her eyes and sleep.

CHAPTER SIXTEEN

Presley would've liked to go see Tess in the morning, but she put it off, knowing she would likely find James at the ranch. Not to mention, she still needed to face her parents and deal with planning how the announcement about her retirement would go.

She ate cottage cheese and strawberries in her kitchenette, before using the connecting door to enter her parents' part of the house.

She hadn't thought about it, but it would make sense for her to move out of the house now. She laughed to herself—it would have made sense for a thirty-year-old to move out long before then, but with the stables on the property it'd always been easier for her to stay. That wasn't the case anymore.

She entered the kitchen to find her parents in an uncomfortable silence. One she was loath to break, but did anyway. "Good morning."

She sat at the table, her hands playing at the cup of coffee she'd carried over from her place.

"Dare we hope you've come to your senses this morning?"

She answered her mother with a small smile. "I told you yesterday that wasn't going to happen."

It was hard for her to blame them for holding out hope that she might change her mind. She had to admit, she almost expected it herself. They didn't know that she'd been thinking about this for a long time. They had no idea that it was some misguided sense of duty to them keeping her in the world of stadium jumping.

And they probably wouldn't understand how her mother's actions had absolved her of that duty. It had, though.

"Presley, this is foolish." Her mother turned to her father. "She's always been like this. She reacts and makes a decision and then there's no changing her mind, but this isn't something we can undo once it's done."

Her mother's words shocked her. Presley wasn't at all like that. She didn't make decisions quickly at all. She obsessed and planned and questioned again and again. It hurt that her mother could be so far off the mark on her.

She wanted to tell them about her plans to open a flower shop, but she didn't. There was no way they would understand that. And she didn't want to subject herself to their arguments that she shouldn't be considering that. She didn't want to subject herself to what would likely be laughter or at the very least scoffing in response. It wouldn't matter that she had a business plan or that she was excited to do it or that she thought she might be really good at it. What would matter was that it wasn't what *they* wanted her to do. It certainly wasn't what was expected of Lawrence and Katerina Royale's daughter.

"Katerina, leave her be. It can be undone if she decides she wants to come back. It can just be a sabbatical. A rest."

Then that was going to be her dad's tactic. To be understanding and give her the time and space she needed to come back to the fold. It was a good strategy, she had to admit. But what he didn't realize was that she wasn't just wanting a little time off. This wasn't about taking a break or not wanting to work hard. She wanted to work hard for something that mattered to *her* now instead of living her mother's and father's dreams.

Her parents argued in the background as Presley began to run through her savings in her head. As one of the top earners in stadium jumping, she'd pulled in a little over a million dollars the previous year, and similar sums for years before that. Of course, the majority of that didn't go to her. It went to Royale Stables.

Most riders kept anywhere from ten to twenty percent of their winnings. Her father had always given her twenty-five percent. Since she lived in her parents' home, she didn't have many expenses.

She bought both her cars with cash over the years. Her education had been paid for by her parents. She didn't have a college degree, but she'd been educated well past the high school level by tutors. To say her life was blessed was putting it mildly.

So she had the kind of savings she needed to start her business. Presley chewed at her bottom lip as she realized what she wanted to do with the day.

"Are you listening, Presley?" Her father's voice pulled Presley from her thoughts.

"I'm sorry, I was thinking."

"I was saying that I realize you don't want to go into training or breeding." She had told them as much the night before, but she was a little surprised to realize her father actually seemed to have absorbed the information. He continued, "but your mother has connections, if you think you might want to go into broadcasting."

Presley blinked. "Broadcasting?"

"Sure, equine sports casting is a field all its own now."

She frowned, unable to fathom why her father thought she would want to go into sports casting. It was the furthest thing from what she might want to do with her life. "I'm sure it's not easy to break into."

"I can put you in touch with the right people." Her mother came and sat at the table, her eyes already sparkling at the idea of it. "I'm sure it's very hard to break in for most people." Her mother waved her hand as though it was understood that Presley was not most people.

Presley shook her head, mostly to clear the fog, but also to remind herself and her parents that she had goals here that mattered. "No. Thank you but no." She took a deep breath. "I have an idea of what I want to do but it's something I need to work on a bit."

It wasn't entirely true. She didn't need to work on her plans for a flower shop. She had the business plan and it had been vetted by other people. She'd run through her budget several times and had even gone so far as looking online at some of the commercial space available in downtown Evers.

What she hadn't done was go look at the available space in person. She would change that today. She didn't want to talk to her parents about what she was doing until she'd put things in motion, though. She wanted to be well enough along in her plans that they understood this was not a whim. That they understood she would not be changing her mind.

She stood, pulling her cell phone out of her pocket. "I'll tell you about it as soon as I can, I promise."

She leaned down and kissed first her father and then

her mother on the cheek, leaving both of them looking a little stunned as she walked out.

She left through the front door, walking around to the back where her cars were. She used her truck when she was doing horsey things, and her Jaguar when she wasn't. It looked like her Jaguar was about to get a lot more use.

CHAPTER SEVENTEEN

Presley asked Laura and Ashley to meet her in town. It was Sunday afternoon, but she was hoping they might be able to get in touch with some of the realtors representing building owners in town.

"What is this all about? You sounded really excited over the phone." Ashley leaned in to hug Presley.

Laura hugged her next and Presley spoke as soon as she released her. "I told my parents I'm retiring."

"Yes! Good for you." Ashley had known Presley had wanted to do this for a long time.

"What?" Laura was a bit more surprised. So far Ashley and James were the only people Presley had ever told about wanting to open a flower shop.

"It's a long story and it's been building for a long time, but for right now I need your help."

"Anything," Ashley and Laura said in near unison.

"I want to look for my space today."

Ashley grinned but Laura shook her head. "It might be a long story, but you're gonna need to back up and give me a little more information. I'm completely lost."

"She's opening a flower shop." The pride in Ashley's voice was almost funny, but Presley did have to admit, it felt really good to hear it.

"And I need to buy a building."

"Buy?" Ashley looked a little stunned. "You're not planning to lease?"

"I will if the right building isn't for sale, but if I can find something for sale, I'd prefer to do that."

"I take it you have savings?" Ashley never was one for dancing around the topic.

"I have very few bills. I've got savings."

Ashley linked arms with Presley and Laura, grinning wickedly as she turned them toward the southern end of the main street in town. "I love shopping, don't you?"

"I've never shopped for a whole building before," Laura said.

Ashley waved a dismissive hand. "It's like buying shoes. Only bigger."

They stopped when they got to the corner and turned back around to face the commercial section of the small town. It was growing. The town had expanded in recent years and the artist studios located in a number of small houses converted to commercial space brought in a fair amount of business. Ashley sat on a committee that had added to the number of festivals the town offered, and those had been growing in popularity and reach as well.

"This looks like trouble."

The women turned to find Haddie Gillman smiling at them with the kind of look that said if they weren't causing any trouble yet, she'd help them remedy that.

Haddie was eighty if she was a day, but she was Ashley's best friend. They filled her in on what they were doing.

"Good for you, girlie," she said with a little pinch to Presley's arm.

"Okay," Laura said. "What does your business plan call for as far as size and location."

Presley didn't need to look at the plan, which she'd tucked away in a file folder in the large tote on her shoulder. She knew it by heart. "I need a space of between seven hundred to one thousand square feet. I'll need to be able to divide the space into the showcase space and then have my design space in the back."

"And I'm willing to bet you know exactly which available spaces fit those needs." Laura grinned.

"I do." Presley smiled at them. She'd never gone so far as to call a realtor and go looking at spaces, but she had checked routinely to see what locations were available for lease or sale in town. "At the moment, there are four empty buildings and two spaces for lease within large buildings. Two of the empty buildings are much too large. Although, I guess I could buy them and try to lease the other space."

Ashley tilted her head. "Then you have to take on the loss until then, not to mention learning how to be a landlord at the same time that you're dealing with becoming a business owner."

"True," Presley said and mentally crossed the two buildings off the list.

"Are you sure you prefer to buy?" Laura asked.

"I think I do," Presley said. "It's unlikely that the business would grow in a small town to the point where I'd need to move into a larger space, so I feel like buying is a good option. And real estate is an investment. If the business doesn't do well, I can sell the space or lease it to someone else."

Ashley jumped in. "Tell us about the two buildings for sale that are the right size."

Presley lifted her hand to point. "There's the house on that side of the street," she said, pointing to a small older house that stood a few doors down from where their friend, Katelyn Davies, had her sculpting studio. "It's close enough to the artists' houses to be considered part of artists' row—" the name had attached itself to the row of houses the artists had turned into studios—"and it's eight hundred and fifty square feet, so it's a good size."

She pointed to the other side of the main street. "Then there's the old convenience store. It's eleven hundred square feet."

Haddie cut in. "Yeah, but it's butt ugly."

"True." Presley looked at the women, who were all nodding their heads in agreement.

The house was old, but it had been painted on the outside. It was a very basic saltbox style house with little charm or character, but she could see about adding a front porch or front eaves or something to add some charm. Even window boxes with flowers would help brighten it up. It was a cheerful light-yellow color that would suit a flower shop well.

The old convenience store was a low squat looking rectangle with a door near one end of the rectangular front. Why the building had been built with no windows, she would never know, but it had been.

"Should we see if we can get a realtor out here to show us them?" Laura asked.

"They're both owned by the Hart brothers," Presley said. The Hart brothers totaled four in number and they hadn't been in the business of buying and leasing property long. Maybe a couple of years.

"Oh, that's better!" Laura said, pulling her phone out. "I'll text Seth. He can't resist May's pies. He'll come out and show us the buildings on a Sunday if I promise him an invitation to Sunday dinner afterward."

And so it was that an hour later, they'd toured through both of the spaces.

Seth, the oldest of the Hart brothers, had said he could talk to his brothers about the possibility of selling one of the buildings rather than leasing them. They stood now, with Seth, in the brick building that had once held a mom-and-pop-style convenience store. It had gone out of business years before when a larger grocery store had opened on the highway between Evers and the next town over.

"I like that this building is larger," Ashley said.

"It's still butt ugly," Haddie put in.

The building was mostly one large room with a small storage space and bathroom at the back.

"True. The house is cute, but with all the small rooms, we'd have to take walls out to open up a large enough display area." Presley looked to Seth. She had told him what she would need before they'd looked at the spaces.

He answered the question before she could ask. "We can take down the walls in the front and open up the living and dining rooms to make a larger space. You can use the kitchen as your work room."

He stepped over to the front wall of the building they were in. "But there's also a lot we can do with this. My brothers and I have talked over a few ideas and planned to make some renovations, but we got tied up flipping a few residential properties." He pointed to the wall that faced the main street in town, where the single entrance door was cut in the corner. "We can break through this wall and put in either one large window along the length of it or even two bay windows, if you'd like. The effect would really add character to the building by getting rid of the boxy shape of it."

Presley nodded and pointed to the shorter wall of the rectangular building. The property was on a corner and this wall faced a small side street. "Can you add a window to this side?"

"Sure. Another bay window might be too much, but maybe two smaller ones to bring in light? You could do window boxes on the outside."

He lifted his clipboard and sketched for a few minutes, before turning the page to her. Laura and Ashley looked over Presley's shoulder, while Haddie pressed in from the side, standing on tip-toe to see.

"Oh I like that," Presley said as the other women nodded their agreement. She pointed to the back of the space where the small storage space and bathroom now stood. "In here, I would need to have you bring the wall of this storage space out some to make the back area bigger. I need a little more space for the work room." She eyed the distance from the front to the back of the building. "Do you know the measurement from front to back?"

Seth looked at his notes. "Says it's twenty-four feet." He took a measuring tape out of a clip on his toolbelt and measured the space as though he would never go only on what a piece of paper said.

He nodded when he'd finished, and Presley calculated in her head. She'd be able to fit the refrigerated display cases along one wall.

She looked to Ashley and Laura who both nodded like it was no big deal to buy a building. Haddie just shrugged her shoulders. Presley looked back to Seth. "Will you talk to your brothers about selling? Look at what you'd want to ask for it."

"You got it," he said, and handed her the clipboard and his pencil. "Write your phone number on there and I'll give you a call sometime tomorrow."

Presley took a deep breath and let it out slowly. She was going to do this. She was really going to do this. And it felt great.

CHAPTER EIGHTEEN

James stood still, Lulu next to his side, pressing her head up into his hand. He'd been doing the exercises Sarah had talked him through when they met, but he couldn't say they were helping him any. Still, he'd see her again next week. He'd give it a shot, if for no other reason than it had finally gotten him off the ranch. Sure, it had been early when there was no traffic and he wouldn't have to see anyone, but still. He laughed as he remembered sitting with Jamie after, talking about the virtues of the sprinkled donut. She had a long list. They could be eaten all at once or one sprinkle at a time, thus suiting any mood (her words, not his). They were soft and melted in your mouth but the added crunch of the sprinkles gave them a nice little boost of texture (again her words, and ones he was pretty sure she'd heard on a cooking show although, likely, not in regards to a donut). And, a sprinkled donut could always bring a smile to your face, she'd added.

She'd said this with a grin, then proceeded to tell him she was hoping her mom and dad had another baby soon because she thought a baby brother or sister would be fun to play with and she could boss it around someday. Her friend, Lily, had a baby brother and she got to tell him what to do. James had said he liked telling his little sister what to do, too. That had earned him a look from Laura.

Lulu's nudge brought James back to the present and he watched as a car pulled into the ranch drive. The silver Jaguar wasn't a car he'd seen before, and it certainly wasn't designed for the ranch, but when it came into view he easily made out the figures inside.

His sister and Presley. His breath caught and held in his chest. When he'd fallen asleep with Presley the night before, he'd known he needed to keep this purely physical between them. She couldn't possibly understand the extent of the damage that had been done to him in the hole he'd lived in for years. She couldn't know that he wasn't ever going to be whole again, wouldn't ever heal.

He should tell her he could seem normal one minute, then the next he'd slip into the inky blackness that could swallow him up for days, and there was no reaching him. He should tell her that one minute he could be standing on Bishop Ranch, sure he was safe, and the next he was flipped upside down and backward, sent back to the jungle where demons and dragons tore at his skin, tore at his soul.

But he didn't tell her.

He needed to back way the hell away from her.

He should have been happy to see she'd left his bed when he woke that morning. Should have been relieved. Should have taken advantage of the escape she'd given him.

"Don't know what the hell is wrong with me," he mumbled to the dog as they walked toward the car.

Laura bounced out of the passenger seat and came toward him. She slipped her arms around him and hugged, pulling back quickly. He hadn't told her it was hard to let people touch him, but she seemed to understand that. All the same, she also didn't seem to be able to resist, but she always pulled away quickly. He understood.

It would have been hell for him to have to think she was dead, and that's what had happened for her. Laura had thought he was dead for over three years. They still hadn't figured out whether their father had been behind the lie or her husband. Laura suspected a little bit of both.

When James had left for the military, their father had been livid. Not because he worried for James at all, but because he was angry they'd both left him. Laura when she married her first husband, Patrick Kensington, and James when he walked into a recruiting office and signed over control of his life for the foreseeable future.

Their father spent his life belittling and neglecting them, only ever paying attention to them when it suited his needs. Like if he wanted someone to demean. It should never have been a shock to the man that both his children walked away as soon as they were able.

Of course, James had gone too soon, it turned out. He buried himself in basic training, then moved into his specialized weapons training before joining the 7th Special Forces Group where he was quickly whisked into special forces training that had him off the grid and out of contact most of the time. He'd left Laura behind, thinking she was safe and happy, but he'd been wrong.

James suspected their father might have called looking for Laura and got Patrick instead. If he said anything remotely like "the boy's dead to me now," which was exactly what his father had been saying at the time, Patrick would have taken that chance to tell Laura her brother was gone.

The man had turned out to be a sick, sadistic son-of-a-bitch. From what Laura's current husband, Cade, had told

James, Patrick then proceeded to beat Laura so badly when she wanted to attend her brother's funeral, she never again questioned where James was buried or when she might be able to visit the grave. She'd been existing in her own hell-hole for years, just trying to stay alive. Just trying not to lose herself to the misery and the terror.

"Presley has exciting news!" Laura said now, pulling back from him.

James had already found his gaze locked onto Presley, so he didn't miss the flush in her cheeks when Laura made her statement.

"News?" He found himself asking. Moments before, he'd been agitated and antsy. Lulu had needed to interrupt the clenching he tended to do with his hands when anxiety hit. She'd interrupted it three times in the last hour, to no avail.

Looking at Presley now, he felt the tightness in his chest ease. He found himself wanting to hear what she had to say. That and so much more. He wanted to go to her, to pull her into his arms. To take her inside.

He didn't.

He stayed glued to the spot while she remained at her car.

"She's opening a flower shop. We went and looked at locations today," Laura said.

"Really?" He asked, not at all missing the spark in Presley's eyes. "Good for you. Did they try to talk you out of it?"

Laura's brow furrowed. "Did who try..." she looked between James and Presley a few times, then shook her head. "James is apparently way ahead of me in the news department," she said, with not a small amount of huffiness to her tone.

She circled around to Presley, hugging her, before

looking back at James with a shake of her head. "I'm just going to leave you two..."

She didn't finish the thought. It didn't matter. The two of them weren't in the least bit focused on Laura. She turned and walked toward her greenhouses on the other side of the driveway.

James repeated his question. "Did they try to talk you out of it?"

He wasn't sure if he made a conscious decision to go to her, but as he waited for her answer, he found he was closer to her.

"I haven't told them yet, but I'm sure they will," she said, the frown on her lips telling him it would hurt to have her parents trying to talk her out of it.

Then he was next to her and for the life of him, he couldn't stop himself from leaning in and kissing one corner of that frown, at the seam where her lips met.

He stood and looked her in the eye, then leaned in and kissed the other side of the frown.

Her mouth opened in a small "oh."

He took her hands and pulled her behind him to the barn, leading the way up into the loft. Every part of him knew this was a piss poor idea. He needed to get his head out of his ass and steer clear of Presley Royale.

But he couldn't. When he'd seen her standing there, next to her car, looking as though she wasn't sure if she should go to him, he'd wanted nothing more than to pull her into him and wrap himself around her.

He'd slept the night before. Really slept. Not for a huge amount of time, but for six hours, which was a hell of a lot longer than he'd slept in a long time.

She hadn't kept the blackness, the nightmares completely at bay. They had come in the night, waking him, but when they had, she'd been there. Her body warm and soft and ready for him. She'd moaned and smiled sleepily at him when he woke her with his body.

She'd kept the darkness from swallowing him and he had the uncontrollable thought that he'd waited forever for her, without ever knowing who she was. She'd somehow been there in his world before he knew she was there. It was a sensation more than a concrete thought. And it was a sensation he couldn't really explain.

He left her standing in the center of the room, then went and closed the shutters on the large window in the loft. It was still early enough that anyone walking on the ranch would see what he was about to do to her.

And no one but him was going to watch as he stripped Presley bare.

He was silent as he moved back to her, running his hands along the line of her neck and up to cup her face as he took her mouth in his. Sweet Jesus, she was heaven on earth. She could make a man *want*, all the while convincing him he could never want for anything again with her in his arms.

She made a small sound in her throat and moved closer, pressing into him as he let his hands drop to run down her back, this time cupping her ass with his hands. He pulled her to him, letting her body meet his. His dick throbbed for her and he needed both of them out of the clothing that separated them.

He reminded himself to be gentle. Her ankle was still weak.

His fingers shook as he worked the buttons of her blouse, then started on her jeans as she removed her arms from the light fabric. His shirt was next, this one coming off over his head. Then he knelt at her feet and tugged her jeans down and off. He stayed there, looking up at his goddess, in her lace panties and bra. She stood, looking down on him, eyes bright and open. She was so damned open. Where she was open, he was closed. Where she was light, he was dark.

"James," she whispered, her hand going to his hair, brushing over it with a touch so light he had to reach for her hand, pulling it against his mouth for a hard kiss. He needed to prove to himself that she was really there. That *he* was really there.

That he really had left the hole. That he'd been pulled out and was safe. He was home.

He pulled his eyes away from her, turning his head and burying his face in her sweet stomach. He clung to her, arms wrapped around her as she ran her fingers through his hair. He didn't know how long they stayed that way before she knelt to face him and wrapped her arms around him.

He wanted to cry but there wasn't anything in him. He was empty and hollow and only Presley could fill him. Only she could fill the blackness of his soul long enough to make him feel, to make him believe that maybe someday he could be whole again.

He lay back, and pulled her down on top of him, running his hands over her, finding the spots on her body that made her moan, that drew the soft mewls of pleasure from her. He made it his mission to make her tremble in his arms. And then he used his mouth and his hands to make her cry out his name.

Somehow in that, he felt anchored, if only for the briefest moment. He knew he would come loose again, floating in that in-between space where he was never sure what was real and what might be imagined. Where he couldn't quite convince himself that the pain was over, that his tormentors were either dead or just too far away to hurt him any longer.

She loved him there on the floor of his loft. Not with her heart or her mind, he knew, but with her body. She stripped him bare, body and soul, and loved him. And he let her, because it was all he could do to keep the pieces of his soul from shattering then and losing himself forever.

CHAPTER NINETEEN

Hours later, they had moved to the bed. Presley lay in James's arms, running her hands up his arms where they wrapped around her. She had the feeling he was with her now, more so than he had been when she'd first arrived. When he brought her to the loft, there had been a desperation to the way he took her. Not the kind of desperation that said he wanted her and couldn't hold back.

This was a soul-deep need to be held by someone. A soul-deep need to feel. To touch. To connect. To connect, even though she would swear he wasn't entirely with her earlier. Wasn't entirely there.

Right now, she was with James and he was there with her.

"Tell me about the spaces you looked at today," he said.

She did. She told him about the little house and the larger building. About the windows Seth had talked about cutting into the brick.

"That sounds like a good plan. The bigger space will be nice."

"It will be," Presley said. "And I don't think it will be

too big. It should be just right."

"Seth is someone you know?"

Presley wished she heard a note of jealousy or tension in him. It was foolish, but she wished that this was something more than it was. His voice was steady, though, holding nothing more than the basic curiosity of a man wanting to know who all the players in the story were.

"Yes, he and his brothers own a building company in town and they own a few properties. He thinks his brothers will be open to selling the building instead of leasing it. If they aren't, I can always lease it and hope they want to sell later."

"Or lease it and buy another space after your business is established."

Presley smiled and let her head rest on his warm arm. The thought of her business being successful made her smile. Would she be thriving and growing in a year?

"Presley," he said, and something in his tone made her still.

"Yeah?" She tried to keep her tone light. Tried like hell to protect herself for what she knew was coming.

"You know I can't give you anything more than this, right? I won't be able to let this be more than just this, what we're doing right now."

Presley nodded, still feeling the warm heat of his skin against her cheek. She didn't need more than he could give her right now. Because, for once, the man she was laying with was being brutally honest with her. He wasn't trying to pretend to be something he wasn't. He wasn't trying to make her believe in something more. He was only telling her exactly what he could offer and what he couldn't.

That meant something to her. No, not something. It meant a lot. A hell of a lot.

CHAPTER TWENTY

Presley padded down the stairs in her bare feet. She must have fallen asleep, but it hadn't been for long. The sun was going down when she woke to find the bed empty beside her.

She could hear James in the barn below, the sound of some kind of saw or sander or something reaching her.

She pushed open the door at the bottom of the stairs and stood watching him. He bent, no shirt covering the muscles of his lean form, running a tool over the top of a bookshelf. She didn't know what the tool was, but she didn't care. The ripple of his skin as his muscles bunched and pulled beneath was entrancing. His arms had started to tan and she guessed it was because he was coming out more. Getting up on Tess and riding in the sun was probably as good for him mentally as it was physically.

Presley stood back, watching from a distance. Somehow, she knew if she walked up to him with the sound of the tool drowning out her approach, she might find herself on the receiving end of a very scary, defensive James.

Instead, she waited, more than happy to enjoy the show.

Lulu stood, leaving her spot next to James, and walked to Presley, inviting petting with a nudge of Presley's hand. That small movement was enough to draw James's attention. He shut off the tool and turned, looking at her as Lulu begged for more petting.

The nerves that danced in her belly under James's gaze threw Presley off and she flicked her eyes to his side to avoid the intensity of his stare. That's when she focused on the shelf he'd been working on.

"It's gorgeous," Presley said, moving forward to inspect the piece. There was nothing typical about it. He'd used wood that wasn't cut into planks with even surfaces and squared-off corners. The wood moved and buckled and flowed with the grain. The front of the shelf had the bark still on the wood. "How do you do this? I mean, how do you get the wood to look like this?"

Tall, dark, and silent guy took her hand and pulled her to a large log laying on its side in another corner of the barn. James lined her up in front of the wood, then wrapped himself around her, his face resting near hers. She could feel his breath whispering over her cheek, and almost had to close her eyes against the sensual assault.

He lifted a chisel and mallet and set the chisel into the wood where a crack already existed. He put the mallet in her hand, then helped her raise it and bring it down on the chisel, splitting the wood with a satisfying crack. He pried the chisel out and moved it further along the crack, repeating the process, until they'd broken off a long piece of the wood.

"It's not very accurate," he said, and she shivered at the feel of his lips on her neck, "but the results are more unique than what I can get if I buy wood that's been run through a mill."

Presley nodded, not really trusting herself to speak.

James held her locked in the teasing trance another moment, then stepped back, breaking the spell and offering a grin.

She shook her head at him. "Tease."

His smile widened, and the lack of remorse was evident.

She moved to another piece he was working on. This one was going to be a large rectangular table, but Presley couldn't figure out how the top of it was going to work. The table frame was wrought iron, welded together in a rectangular shape with sturdy legs. Set into the tabletop were three large logs that had clearly been split in the method he'd just shown her.

The bottom of the logs was rounded and still held the bark of the tree on them. The tops of the logs—the portions that had been split—had been sanded smooth, but still held the ripples of the wood where it had split. They were anything but flat. And they'd been set down in the table by a few inches.

James came up behind her and ran his hand over the top edge of the table. "After I get them smooth and stain them to draw out the pattern of the grain of the tree, I'm going to fill this in with resin to give the tabletop the flat surface it needs. You'll still see the grain of the tree through the resin." He shrugged. "I think it will work."

Presley looked at him, stunned to see that he didn't think much of what he was doing. "This is incredible, James. It's stunning."

"I think Laura will like it."

"It's for Laura?"

He nodded. "For her greenhouse."

Presley looked back at the shelf and the table, then turned to him. "Would you build my display shelves for the flower shop? The way you keep the wood looking so natural, but adding a finished look to it would be perfect for the shop."

He held her look for a minute before glancing down. "If you can bring me pictures or videos of the space, take the measurements for me. I can't go there with you, Presley."

The tears that pressed at her eyes surprised her with how swiftly they came, how fast the pain hit her. It killed her knowing he couldn't do something as simple as taking a drive with her into town to tour her building. Laura had told her James didn't leave the ranch, but this was the first time she'd had to face it.

She pasted a smile on her face, knowing it was entirely too bright, too big. "No problem. I've got tons of pictures and videos already and I can get more if you need them."

James stepped away, pretending to study something on the table top, examining one of the corners and running his thumb over it.

She stood still for a minute, not at all sure how to handle this. He knew she'd been feeling pity for him and she hated that. It wasn't pity, exactly. It was anger and pain and hopelessness. She was hopeless to know how to fix this for him, but that's what she wanted. And she realized then that that was foolish. She could never fix this for him. All she could do was accept him as he was and be there for him when he needed her.

She stepped over to him, slipping between his body and the table. Her hands ran over his chest and up to rest on his shoulders, and his eyes met hers, pain and a bleak emptiness evident.

"James," she said, looking back toward the table then back again, "these are incredible. They're unique and special and perfect in their imperfection. I would love it if you would make something like this for me for the flower shop. Please?"

Something in his gaze filled and the emptiness wasn't complete any longer. It was still there, but it was no longer all that was there. He nodded and then he lifted her and brought her back to his loft.

When he made love to her this time, Presley clung to the hope that maybe she could fill the empty space inside of him a little bit, at least for a short time. If she could give him that, she gladly would. Even if it meant she would walk away from this. It would hurt like hell when she had to walk away, but she'd give him that if that's all she could do for him.

CHAPTER TWENTY-ONE

"Okay," Ashley said. "Phoebe is making the margaritas and Katelyn is bringing the cookies in just a minute."

Phoebe Joy was dating Laura's brother-in-law, Shane, and Katelyn Davies was married to Sheriff John Davies and owned one of the artist studios in town.

Ashley set a tray with chips and queso on the coffee table that sat in front of the couch Laura and Presley shared. The doorbell rang, but before Ashley could answer it, her sister Cora popped the front door open and called out. "It's just me!"

Cora was trailed by her other sister, Emma, and a smiling Lily Winn, the town veterinarian who was married to one of the deputies who worked for Katelyn's husband.

The group of women was tight-knit, and Presley was always glad Ashley had brought her under her wing and introduced her to them all. Presley was always the quiet one in any group, probably a result of the fact she'd been socially isolated a lot of her life, but she didn't feel like an outsider with these women anymore.

As the group settled in around her and Phoebe came

out of the kitchen passing margaritas around, Ashley called out to everyone from the head of the room. "Okay, ladies. I'm going to do the announcing for Pres because, well, we all know she won't brag and I will. On that note, let me be the first to introduce you to the new owner of Petals and Posies, a new flower shop that's going to be located in the old convenience store building downtown. Presley just found out the Hart brothers have accepted her bid to buy the building."

Ashley raised her glass in a toast and the women all turned to congratulate Presley, making her cheeks flush. Despite her embarrassment, it felt good to be surrounded by friends who she knew would be cheering her on through the whole thing. These women would have her back.

"Tell us everything," Katelyn said.

Presley laughed. "Everything?"

"Her business plan is solid," Lily said. "I've seen it and she has everything covered."

"When do you plan to open?" Katelyn asked.

"I think in two months. I still need to finalize the buildout with Seth, so I might build in a little cushion and make it three months."

"You know," Katelyn said, "that building is so close to the artists' studios, we could probably include you in the artists' walk map. Do you have any blank wall space where you could feature an artist each month or every other month? It might bring people in who might end up purchasing something or coming back to you when they need flowers for an event."

Presley set down her drink. "That's a great idea. And, yes, I think I could leave some space for that. I have one wall devoted to the refrigerated display cases that will hold pre-made bouquets and stem flowers. James is going to make me some floating shelves to go on some of the other walls, but there's certainly space to install a few pieces."

Ashley pointed to Presley. "And that brings us to the next thing I wanted to ask about. Tell us all about James," she said, drawing out the word *all*. "What's going on between you two?"

Cora laughed and clapped her hands. "We want details."

Laura stuck her fingers in her ears. "We really don't. We really, really don't."

Cora tossed a pretzel at Laura. "Speak for yourself. Some of us have no dating life. We need to live through others."

It was well known in the group that the only person Cora was interested in dating was Justin Kensington, Laura's former brother-in-law through her first marriage. Sadly, although he now lived in Evers and worked with Laura, the man seemed determined to live like a monk.

"James is my brother," Laura said, throwing the pretzel back with a laugh. "I don't need any details. Or even vague information. I need to know absolutely nothing whatsoever about his dating life."

Presley raised her hands. "We're not dating. Not at all. He's really not in a place for that, guys." They didn't need to know about the sex. What was happening with James was complicated. It wasn't really something she could explain to them.

The room quieted. What had happened to James in South America was no secret.

"How's he doing?" Ashley asked, looking to Laura for her answer.

Laura looked like she was struggling with how to

answer. She finally went with, "He's getting a little better each day I think?"

She looked to Presley, who nodded. "He has good days and bad. I think it's the kind of thing where he takes a step forward then a step back and so on, but I think he's getting better." She nodded again at Laura, as though if she nodded enough, she could reassure her friend.

She didn't say that James still couldn't leave the ranch, except to go to therapy. That he woke shivering in the night. That he sometimes blacked out in the middle of a conversation and didn't seem to come back to himself for hours at a time. She knew Laura knew some of that. Obviously, she saw that James didn't leave the ranch, but she didn't know how much of the rest of it Laura knew.

"He told me he feels like a failure," Laura said. "He feels guilty for not keeping me away from Patrick, for not realizing what was happening."

Emma spoke, then. "What I've never understood is how you didn't know where he was. Why didn't you know James was in the military at all?"

Laura had only found out James was in the military when Phoebe and Shane had tracked him down three months before.

"Emma!" Cora said and Ashley laughed. It was usually Cora and Emma who scolded Ashley for saying the wrong thing or asking forward questions.

Emma folded her arms over her chest. "What? It's not like you all didn't want to ask."

Laura sighed and tucked her feet under her. "I haven't talked to James about it, but one of his friends he served with sat down with me when James was in the hospital."

"Jeff Hunt?" Presley asked, remembering the man who had visited James.

"Yes, he was really great. I know most people who served in the kinds of places they've been to don't want to talk about it, but Jeff reached out to me to see if I had questions. He seemed to know James wouldn't be able to talk to me about that kind of stuff."

"They were in basic together," Presley said, more to the group than to Laura.

Laura nodded. "They went into special forces together afterwards. Jeff said in special forces they had a minimum of three years of training, some of the guys had more. The training exercises were all over. He and James basically left basic and their Army Individual Training, and went right into their Q course together. It's the qualification course for special forces. They split off from there, each going into specialized courses, but then came back to the 7th Special Forces Group together. They were shipped out of the country for training ops that could last months at a time. James would keep up with me through email on the occasional times he had access to write, but I never saw those. By that time, Patrick had taken over my account and was responding to James for me. I think that's one of the reasons James is so hard on himself. He didn't realize it wasn't me writing back to him and he thinks he should have."

"Don't forget, he would have seen you in the news when he could get news from the states. He would have no reason to think you weren't okay," Cora said.

When Laura had been married to Patrick Kensington, she'd lived her life in a fishbowl as part of the Kensington dynasty. A family of Senators and high-powered business-men, they were seen in the news and at events on a regular basis. Laura had been very good at hiding her shame—and her bruises—from the world.

Laura's next words looked like they cost her a lot to say,

and she was used to talking about her past. "Patrick convinced me James was dead about six months into our marriage." None of the women needed the explanation for that. They knew Patrick had controlled everything Laura did, everyone she talked to. "From what we were told by the Army, James wasn't captured until almost two years after that. Patrick convinced him for all that time, that it was me answering those emails, but I never blamed James for not figuring it out. Patrick was incredibly manipulative. He knew how to convince people of anything." Laura finally said.

"I'm sorry. I really didn't mean to bring things down," Emma said.

"Hey, I wanted to hear about nookie," Cora said, raising her hands and bringing back a much-needed lightness to the conversation.

Presley grinned. "I'm not talking about it. But he is going to build some display shelves and the checkout counter for the flower shop."

"He builds things?" Ashley asked.

Laura nodded. "There was some old wood-working stuff in the barn and he took to it. It's been good for him to have something to do."

"And his style is going to be perfect for the shop," Presley said.

"Tell us more about your grand opening plans, Pres," Lily said.

"Actually, I wanted to get your opinion of something. I was reading a blog about small businesses and several of the people commenting had been successful with offering something free for the first month. Most of them were the type of place that offers classes, like an exercise place or a gymnastics school. For the first month they were open, they filled their classes with people and gave them away free. When they started charging, they had full rosters and were able to maintain that over time. I was brainstorming a way to apply that to the flower shop. What do you think of free flowers for the first week I'm open? It would cost a good chunk of money, and obviously I would limit it to a few of the smaller designs I've got planned and only one per customer, but I thought it might get people in the door."

The women seemed to consider it and Katelyn grinned. "I like it. You could run ads promoting it as a romantic gesture. Like, *swing by and grab a bouquet for your loved one* kind of thing. Then the men see that their women like the flowers and maybe they come back."

"Or the women get them for their men," Emma said, pertly.

"Or a woman brings one home to her woman," Ashley said.

"So you like it?" Presley asked.

The women all murmured their agreement.

"You'll need to decide how to advertise it and how far and wide you want to advertise it," Lily said. Her experience as a small business owner was turning out to be a big help. "If you have ten percent of the population of Evers take you up on the offer, that's one thing, but ten percent of Evers plus three or four of the surrounding towns might be another."

"You could always do something like limit it to the first fifty customers and offer anyone after that a coupon for a percentage off," Ashley said.

"People like coupons where they get to spin a wheel or choose from a hat. They might get ten percent off, or they might get twenty or five," Emma said.

"And get their email and mailing addresses as part of the deal," Lily said. "Build your mailing list."

Presley had pulled her phone out and was tapping notes. Some of this she'd thought of and some she hadn't. She'd been taking an online course on newsletter marketing and knew she needed to start building her contact list right from the start. She couldn't picture a big spinning wheel for the coupons in her store, but they could pick a coupon out of a flower pot or something cute like that.

They spent the next hour tossing around ideas for her grand opening and she got the names of a couple of artists who might do her logo for the shop. After that, things devolved as the margaritas flowed and several cartons of ice cream made an appearance. All the while, Presley grinned at the thought that she didn't need to say no to any of it. Sure, she wanted to stay healthy, but she no longer had to maintain the body of an athlete. Nor did she have to run home and get to bed because she had a show to get up for at four in the morning.

Her life, for once, was all hers.

CHAPTER TWENTY-TWO

"Hey, Dad." Presley stood in the doorway of the observation room in the indoor riding ring. It was a long room in one corner of the ring that had windows facing the ring, letting viewers watch anyone riding in the ring in a comfortable, climate controlled space. There were couches and a refrigerator, and even a television mounted in one corner of the ceiling.

It was the last place Presley expected to find her father. He was usually out in the center of the ring, shouting instructions to his pupils. The observation room was for parents and riders who were waiting for their lessons.

His gaze was distracted when he turned to her, but he offered a small smile. It was all the greeting she was going to get.

Presley turned to see who he was watching but the ring was empty.

"You okay, Dad? I went up to the house, but Mom wasn't home."

He continued to stare at the ring and she wondered

what he was seeing in his mind's eye. "Your mother went to stay in the New York apartment for a while."

"What?" Presley looked at her father, willing him to look at her instead of the empty arena. She'd often wondered what their relationship would have been like if she hadn't been a good rider. What if she'd had a clue when she took her first jump on a horse that she might fall and break her neck? What if she'd been afraid instead of riding hell bent for leather over that first obstacle? Would she have seen much of her dad?

Who knows, maybe she wouldn't have seen as much of him, but maybe their relationship would have been a softer one, instead of one where he pushed her to the brink time and time again, always pressing her to be the best, to do better, to reach farther.

"Dad?" She prompted when he didn't answer. They only used the New York apartment when they were in the northeast for shows. Her mother had never gone there on her own before.

He turned, looking only briefly at her before moving to sit on one of the leather couches. "Your mom's going to stay in New York for a little while. We, uh," he ran a hand through his hair, "we haven't been getting along all that well since the incident with the horse. I'm going to talk to Harry and Davenport's owner. I have to see if we can make this right, but I want to try to do it in a way that keeps your mom from . . ."

He didn't finish, but she got what he was saying. He didn't want her mom to have to face any consequences for what she'd done. Presley couldn't help but think that maybe her mom needed to face the consequences of her actions for once. Still, she understood all too well what this would do. If this got out, her dad's career, everything he loved and worked for, would likely be destroyed. Her mother's actions might take them all down.

Harry cared about the well-being of the horses. If they couldn't convince him her mother wouldn't act in a way that could harm them again, he wouldn't go along with trying to settle the matter quietly, no matter how much money her parents threw at him and Davenport's owner.

She didn't know what to say, so she sat, putting her hand on her dad's arm. Why was it so hard to talk to him? Why was it hard to just be there for him?

Because you have no relationship beyond riding, a little voice in her head said, and Presley had to blink to fend off the tears that pricked at her eyes. It was true. There were no memories of family vacations, no happy Christmas mornings, no kissing her dad goodbye as she left for her prom. The trips they'd gone on had been to horse shows, or occasionally, to visit a horse her father was thinking of buying.

Her mother and her had taken shopping trips from time-to-time, jetting to Milan or London or Paris for a week to satisfy her mother's urge to find the latest fashions. But her father never went on those trips. In fact, more often than not, neither did Presley. They interfered too much with her riding schedule.

Christmas mornings had been quiet in her house. She was an only child, so she'd opened her gifts with her parents watching from the couch as they sipped their coffee before her father and her went out to the stable to ride.

And the prom. Well, that hadn't happened at all. She'd been homeschooled by tutors who traveled with her when she went to compete or when she was away training with her team in preparation for the nationals or the Olympic games.

Her dad put his hand over hers and smiled at her again.

"It's all right. We just needed a little break from each other while I try to work through all this. She'll be back soon."

Presley nodded, but she felt sick to her stomach. It was silly, really, and she was probably overreacting. It was silly to feel the sudden panicky need to know her parents were going to be okay. That they would be happy and together, and that they'd be that way for a long time. That nothing would change with them.

Was it selfish that she wanted to be able to change her own life, but didn't want them to change at all?

She leaned against her father and put her arms around his strong arm. He leaned over and kissed the top of her head and Presley closed her eyes. The movement was small and almost meaningless. Except that it was something he'd never done before.

CHAPTER TWENTY-THREE

Presley sat crossed-legged on James's bed, trying to focus on the software in front of her. She was working her way through the tutorial exercises for the software she would use to run her business. It would do everything from helping her plan out orders for people, to designing the arrangements. It let her check out walk-in clients and create detailed invoices for larger orders. She could also use it to schedule and manage orders and her delivery calendar. And if she didn't keep her eyes off James, she wasn't going to learn how to use it anytime soon.

James stood in the center of the space, hands taped and gloved, chest and shoulders glistening with sweat, as he hit a large weight bag over and over. He'd been at it for thirty minutes and it was still mouthwatering to watch.

She looked back at her computer. She had ten more slides to read in the training section she was on, then she planned to look through the real estate listings. It was time for her to find a place to live downtown. Her family's home and stables sat on a large stretch of land that was twenty minutes outside of Evers. She could commute if she needed to, but it made more sense for her to move closer. Besides, now that she didn't have the excuse of being close to the barn for the horses, it was more than a little lame for her to be living in her parents' house, even if she was in the in-law suite.

She looked back up at James, who hadn't broken his focus on the bag. She was pretty sure he was going to punch a hole right through to the other side of it, but she didn't mind the show. He was intense and sexy as sin. He seemed to go into a zone when he did this, but not in the way he sometimes did when he seemed to blackout, leaving himself and her for a time and falling into a trance that could be scary to watch. No, this was different.

She had been spending more and more time in the loft with him. It would be tempting to fantasize that they might be moving toward living together, with all the time they spent in bed at his place, but she wouldn't let herself go there. She wasn't foolish enough to spin that little web of lies for herself. Not again.

James froze, arms in mid punch, and she would swear he wasn't breathing. In a flash, he was moving again, stripping off his gloves and struggling to tear the tape from his hands as he moved to the bedside table.

She recognized it and stayed still as he dove for his journal and pen. He scribbled for several minutes before sitting back and holding the journal in his lap. She'd seen him like this when he woke from dreams.

Other times, he wouldn't wake. He would talk in his sleep, mentioning names. *Silva, Catalina.* Lulu would wake him and he'd hold the dog. Twice, he'd turned to hold Presley instead of the dog.

"What is it?" She asked now. "Did you remember more?"

It had taken a long time for him to tell her what he was writing and she hadn't pressed. She knew that wasn't the kind of relationship he wanted from her.

He nodded.

"Do you want to tell me about it?"

He shook his head, but put the journal back on the table and turned to crawl to her. She hadn't looked on purpose, but she couldn't help but see the word *guns* and the word *crates* scrawled on the page.

Presley squealed when he came down over her, pushing her laptop out of the way. He lay on her, sweaty body and all, laughing and capturing her mouth with his own.

She wrinkled her nose. "You're so sweaty."

He growled. "We'll shower when we're done."

Presley laughed but fell silent when his mouth moved down her throat and he wrapped one arm around her, using it to shift her down the bed till she lay on her back. And then he was over her and the distraction was complete. Sweaty or not, it didn't matter. All that mattered was his touch and the way he made her feel. The way he made her come apart in his arms.

CHAPTER TWENTY-FOUR

James let his hand linger on Presley's leg when he gave her a leg up into the saddle.

"Feel good?"

She smiled down at him. "It does. I missed this." Her ankle was fully healed, and she was happy to be back on Tess.

James mounted a rescue horse Cade had rehabbed next to her.

He raised a brow at her. "Second thoughts on retiring?"

"Not at all." Presley turned Tess and led her out over the worn path through the back of the property. Cade had told them the trail would lead to a small pond and an open field where they could picnic. Cade's mother had whipped up a homemade lunch that had made Presley's mouth water as she watched everything being packed into the little cooler backpack James had slung on his shoulders.

Tess wasn't thrilled to be following along behind James's horse, but Presley was happy for the chance to watch James from the back. She pressed her lips together as she focused on the sight of his muscles rippling beneath his t-shirt. There was something to be said for a no-strings-attached, this-can't-go-anywhere relationship based solely on sex. If a little piece of her insisted she was lying as she had the thought, she shoved that piece aside. She was going to enjoy this. End of story.

"Cade thinks he might have a home for Jelly Bean," James said, referring to the horse he rode.

"I still think that's an utterly ridiculous name for a horse that's anything bigger than fourteen hands," Presley said. "But I'm glad to hear he might have a home for him. Unless you wanted to keep him for yourself."

James only offered a shrug in response and she wondered if he was resisting the urge to tie himself to anyone or anyplace. Even though he was living on the ranch, there was a very temporary feel to him. She had tried, recently, to let herself feel what he might be feeling, and she had come to the conclusion that maybe it was hard for him to trust in any of this. That maybe he didn't want to believe that he could have a life where he was safe and didn't have anything to fear.

She didn't say anything for the rest of the ride out to the pond and he didn't seem to feel the need to break the silence either. James was like that, always happy to let silence stretch on when others, including herself at times, might feel the need to fill it.

They circled to the backside of the pond before stopping and settling in for lunch.

"I really don't take advantage of May's offers to cook for me enough," James said as he set the food onto the blanket Presley had spread on the ground.

Presley's stomach rumbled in response and she pressed a hand to it, laughing. "My stomach agrees."

There was chicken salad, cut apples, and chunks of

cheese. Presley opened one container and smiled. "Pie. She packed apple pie."

James laughed as Presley loaded her plate high.

"Don't laugh at me," she scowled. "I'm taking advantage of my retirement. I can eat whatever I want now."

"You had a strict diet?"

Presley nodded, her mouth too full of chicken salad to answer.

"Makes sense, I guess, but I hadn't really thought about it. I would have thought you kept in shape with all the riding and wouldn't have had to worry about gaining weight with all the calories your training schedule burned."

She shrugged. "I guess I'm about to find out how many extra calories my figure can handle without hours of riding in a day."

James just shook his head and laughed, digging into his own plate.

When they'd finished, neither one of them wanted to go anywhere and the horses seemed content to graze on grass while James stretched out. He laid his head on Presley's legs, taking her arm and wrapping it around his torso.

They lay together in silence for a long time before he spoke. In a completely uncharacteristic move, he began to talk about his feelings. He went almost exactly to the thoughts she'd had as they rode to the pond, as though he'd read her mind.

"I worry, sometimes, that this might all go away. That something will happen to take away everything." He didn't say *again* but it was there, nonetheless, and she thought of how many times he'd lost everything.

His mom first, although he probably wasn't old enough to remember much about her when she died. She didn't know much about his childhood, but from what Laura had told her, she and James had been close, relying on each other when their father's cruelty got to be too much. Then Laura had married and left him. As happy as he'd probably been for her, it had to hurt to be left behind.

He'd built a career in the military, then, albeit a short one. And then his whole life had been taken. For years, his freedom, his safety, and likely some of his sanity had been ripped out from under him.

"Why do you say that?" Presley asked, running her fingers through his hair.

"I guess you get used to waiting for the bad to come."

The statement made her ache for him. "Tell me about some of the bad."

She didn't think he would, but he surprised her.

"I fell in love over there, in the Devil's Den."

Presley stilled for a minute but forced herself to relax. She had heard the small region he was held in was called the Devil's Den. There was little government control there. It was a vicious and violent region.

"When they took me, I was injured."

She knew that. He'd told her he didn't remember any of the battle where he was captured. It was why he wrote in his journal, trying to piece together flashes and images as they came to him. Presley held still, reminding herself to breathe, forcing herself to be silent. She didn't want to stop him from talking if this was what he needed.

"I was taken first by one of the leading drug cartels in the area, led by a man named Peña."

"Not Silva?" She asked.

He looked surprised she knew the name.

"You say his name in your sleep sometimes." She didn't mention that he called for Catalina more often.

James shook his head. "Silva didn't have me for a while.

When I was first captured, I was hurt so bad, Peña didn't have much use for me. Didn't know if I'd live long enough to be of any use."

She thought of the scars on his legs, scarring from burns going up to the thighs. She knew James had no memory of the events, but Hunt had told him he'd been in a building that had blown up. Hunt and Lars didn't think James could have survived the explosion. The whole building had been destroyed. But when backup arrived and they went in to find the bodies of their squad mates, they'd found everyone but James.

Presley kept her fingers running through his hair, again and again, the repetition soothing.

James looked confused for a minute. "Peña was there, but so was Silva."

"You remember that?"

He shook his head, brow furrowed, and she knew it frustrated him to be missing so many details about that day. "I remember Silva's voice, but Peña had me when I was first taken, so he must have been there."

He stared into space for several minutes, and she thought he was finished until he spoke again.

"Peña gave me to a woman in the jungle to heal. She was old and people said she was a witch, but I think she was just good with medicine. She knew how to find what she needed in the land she lived off. She and her granddaughter kept me for months in their home, treating my injures and nursing me back to health."

So they could torture him, she thought. It was sick to heal someone, only so you could break them again, wasn't it?

"Catalina," he said, almost a whisper.

"That was the woman?" Presley asked, breaking her silence.

"Her granddaughter." He didn't say anything more and she didn't ask. He seemed to have taken the story as far as he wanted it to go for the moment, but she wondered if Catalina was the woman he'd loved.

Where was Catalina now, she wondered? More, though, she wondered if James still loved Catalina, and if he could ever love another. Because heaven help her, she wanted him to whisper her name that way. With reverence and an ache that said he wasn't quite whole without that person. Heaven help her, she wanted that because it was how she'd started to feel for him. Like when this was over, she wouldn't be quite whole.

CHAPTER TWENTY-FIVE

A week later, James watched as Presley walked across the field to him. She wasn't limping any longer and wasn't wearing her air cast. If she'd seen him, she made no indication of it. He leaned against the door to the barn and watched the sun hit her face. Presley was everything beautiful and light in the world. He wanted to reach out and touch her, let that beauty and light seep into his soul and make him strong again.

He saw the instant she noticed him. Her eyes flashed brighter and a smile broke onto her features. Something inside of him whispered that he didn't deserve her. That he should push her far away before he tarnished her with who and what he was, but he wasn't strong enough to do that. At some point, he'd begun to need Presley Royale.

When she got to where he stood, he reached out and tugged her to him, wrapping himself around her as he bent his head to rest on hers.

"You feel good," she said, tipping her head back and looking up at him. He liked that he didn't have to bend much to drop a kiss to her lips. She was tall and strong. His match in so many ways.

He kissed her deeply, then leaned back to catch the dazed look she probably didn't know she had whenever he kissed her like that. He liked watching her that way.

"I have things to show you today," he said.

Presley grinned lasciviously at him. "Oh yeah?"

And then he was laughing and the lightness he'd wanted to harness from her had come, however fleeting, into him. "Not that kind of show and tell, although we can save that idea for later."

He took her hand and pulled her inside, watching as she bent to greet Lulu.

James led Presley to his work area, where he'd been playing around with ideas for her shop. He lifted a section of log he'd quartered, this time using a saw to make the cut so he ended up with two flat surfaces and a rounded surface that still had the bark on it. He went to the wall and held the log up against it.

"I was thinking we could mount pieces like this as floating shelves around the space," he said as she came over to look at it. "I can stain them in whatever color you want or even just oil them and leave them natural."

"I love that." She reached out and ran her fingers over the grain where he'd sanded it down.

"Good." It was ridiculous how happy it made him feel to make her happy. He set down the log and pulled her over toward the table he'd been working on for Laura. "I finished this," he said, hoping she would like the way the table had turned out.

She ran her hands over the top of it, feeling the smooth surface of the resin.

"It's beautiful, James! I can't believe you made this."

He grinned. "I was thinking I can do something similar for your workspace. I can make it larger so it's big enough for more than one person to work at it when you get to the point where you need that. I have a few ideas for custom elements we can do on it."

"Show me," she said, and he flashed again to the idea of show and tell with Presley. Damn, she was going to be the death of him.

He put his hand on the wide bands of metal he'd used to frame out the table top. "If I frame the table with this, then we can also make some small rectangle shapes with the metal and set it into the top before I pour the resin. It will give you cups to store things like scissors and whatever else you need when you're working."

"Oh, I like that idea."

He went on, pointing to the outer edges of the table. "I was also thinking, I can add a strip around the edges of the table, maybe three inches wide." He held his hand out at the edge to show her. "I'd make them slanted runners, open at the top and then with an opening at the bottom of each corner of the table. You would be able to push any scraps from your work down into the runner around the edge and the slant would make it easy to push all the scraps down to the opening at the corner and right into a trash can."

She didn't answer this time with words. She came and wrapped her arms around him and crushed him in a hug.

James laughed. "You like that idea?"

"I love it!"

She'd been ordering supplies for the shop the other day and had told him that the workspace in the back would be filled with wet and slippery stems from the cuttings. She'd need nonslip mats under her feet and would have to sweep up the cuttings regularly. She'd still need the mats, but this would make it a lot easier for her to keep the space clean.

Now for the really scary part. "I was thinking, I want to go see the building with you."

"You do?" She couldn't hide the surprise in her voice.

He nodded. "I can't promise I'll make it. We might get out on the road and I'll need to come running back, but I want to try." He didn't add the *running back like a baby* part of his thoughts.

"That's okay. You do what you can." She didn't say it like she thought there was anything wrong with a grown man who couldn't leave his home. Not even his home, a home he was living in for free because there wasn't any way he could hold down a job.

"Can we try to go today?"

She nodded. "And you need to tell me what I need to budget for the table and shelves and things."

"Nothing. You don't need to pay me for them. It gives me something to do."

"Nonsense." Her hands went to her hips as she schooled him. "Of course, I'm paying you for your work. It's incredible. You could make pieces like this for a living, especially if you custom design them for people like you're doing for me."

James took a step backward and scowled. "Yeah, sure, I could charge people and then have a breakdown in the middle of their project and not be able to deliver in time. That'll go over well."

She was forgetting the fact he sometimes stopped working for days, hiding upstairs in the loft. Either that, or she was choosing to ignore that little reality.

"You're an artist. People can put up with whatever they

need to from an artist if the work is good enough. And this is."

She came forward, hands going to his shoulders. He felt the anger that seemed to rip through him at times with no warning and no reasonable connection to anything that was happening. It was an overreaction, pure and simple.

"Stop it, Presley. Don't baby me. I am what I am and there isn't anything that's going to change that, so you need to stop thinking you can."

She kept her face calm and waited while he yelled. He didn't want to see the patience she was giving him. It wasn't something he deserved. Why didn't she yell and tell him what an ass he was?

Lulu came and stood next to him, pressing into his leg. The dog didn't deserve this either, he knew. He suspected Cade had taught the dog to handle sudden yelling and screaming, but still, she didn't deserve what he put her through.

He couldn't stop it, though. Whenever the anger hit like this, it hit hot and hard, running through his blood like lava.

He picked up the floating shelf he'd made her only minutes before and threw it against the wall, the sound satisfying in the dim light.

Darkness. He was better in the dark. He should live there and never try to come out of it.

"Go away, Pres." He didn't yell the words, but they were hard and angry, and they should have frightened her into retreat.

He heard her footsteps as she turned to walk away, but she didn't go far enough. When he turned, it was to see her sitting on one of the chairs, ignoring him and looking at one wall of the barn. She was staying close, but letting him have his rage.

James fell to his haunches, kneeling and letting his head fall to his hands. What the hell was wrong with him?

He tipped his head back and roared his anger for long minutes, before letting his head fall back to his hands. Sometimes, the anger that overtook him scared him. He didn't know how to handle it. The lessons Sarah had taught him weren't automatic enough to come to him at times like this.

He didn't know how long they stayed like that. It might have been twenty minutes, or two hours. At some point, Lulu came to him, pressing her head to his hand. He sat back, landing on the wood floor, and let her crawl into his lap. He held the dog and waited for the emotions to ebb.

In time, Presley stood and came to him, holding out her hand and walking with him to the loft when he took it.

Going to the flower shop would have to wait for another day. He wasn't ready for that yet.

CHAPTER TWENTY-SIX

James waited a few days before bringing up the trip to her flower shop again.

"Maybe we can go to the building today? I want you to show me where you want things and I need to take some measurements." He said this as casually as he could. He didn't know if she'd still be willing to try it with him. Hell, he'd been surprised she stayed with him.

The last thing he wanted to do was be abusive to Presley or take advantage of what she offered him. She was there whenever he needed her and she'd stayed there throughout the whole episode. It was more than he deserved.

His father had been an abusive ass when he was growing up. He rarely hit James and Laura, but his mood swings and drinking had been abusive, all the same. He'd cut into them with words that hurt in ways punches couldn't. If they hadn't had each other growing up, things would have been ugly.

James didn't want that for Presley. She deserved better than him. One of these days, he was going to need to send her away. To tell her she needed to find a man worthy of her. He was a selfish asshole for not doing that now. But he swore to himself, if he saw he was acting like his dad, he'd cut her out of his life rather than hurt her the way his dad had hurt him and Laura.

"We can do that," she said, with a smile, taking his hand in hers. He loved it when she did that. Her hand was strong, but smaller than his. He liked the way the brush of her skin against his felt as he wrapped his fingers around hers. "When do you want to go?"

The conversation was feeling all too reminiscent of the one that had taken place right before his rage the other day. It made his skin itch like it was too tight. "Now?" He wanted to do this before he chickened out.

She just smiled, eyes dancing with excitement as she grabbed her purse. "Let's go."

When they got to the car, James realized he needed to drive. He had thought he'd sit in the passenger seat and work on keeping his breathing steady but that hadn't worked all that well with Laura when she took him to the therapist. By the time he'd gotten to his appointment, he'd been in physical pain from the tension in his body.

It hit him suddenly that he needed the control of being behind the wheel. He hadn't had that when Laura drove, but he had a feeling if he could get behind the wheel, it would make a difference.

"Can I drive?"

If she thought anything of the request, she didn't say so. "Sure." She pointed to the driver's side as she moved to the passenger's side. "Just push the button to start the car."

It occurred to him then that she was turning over a Jaguar to him. This wasn't an old clunker.

Then he remembered he had Lulu by his side. The

thought of leaving the ranch without her made him sick to his stomach. He looked around. Cade had an old Jeep by the other barn. Maybe they could find him and ask to borrow that.

Presley apparently wasn't concerned. She opened the back door and called to Lulu who hopped in and circled twice before settling.

He slid into the leather seats and took a deep breath.

"You good?"

He nodded and looked at the dash. He'd been surprised to see the push button start in his sister's car, but she'd told him most cars had it now. The things a guy could miss when he was trapped in a hole wondering if he'd be fed in time to live another day, he thought.

He put his foot on the brake, pushing the button to start the car.

He half expected Presley to take an oh-shit grip on the car as he drove, but she leaned back in her seat, looking nothing more than excited to have him with her.

James braked at the end of the ranch's drive and laughed, drawing a look from Presley.

"I have no idea where I'm going," he said looking to the left, then the right.

She shook her head and laughed with him, pointing to the left. "Follow this road for twenty minutes. Takes you right into town."

James breathed deeply as they drove, feeling antsy as he watched the ranch recede in his rear-view mirror. He could do this. And then Presley was talking to him, telling him about the progress at the store, how the workers had cut through the brick and were framing out the windows. She talked about what flowers would be available at good prices during her grand opening based on the season and which suppliers were close by.

She told him about the paint colors she'd chosen for the walls—which to him sounded like variations of off-white but to her seemed to mean something else—and she talked about her logo which was almost ready.

Then, they were approaching the town and he was okay. Not fantastic, but okay. There hadn't been any flash-backs, He didn't spiral off into blackness.

She pointed to a side street coming up. "Turn off here and then head south for a few blocks."

He did what she said and realized she was taking him around into the residential streets that surrounded the town. She gave him a few more directions, and they were pulling up to a brick building through a small alley at the back entrance.

She'd taken him around so he didn't need to drive through the town, he realized.

Someday, he wanted to stand on the front sidewalk and look up at her building and see her logo there and the flower boxes he planned to build to go outside her windows. He would do it, but today, he was grateful she'd realized he needed to come in the back.

The back door was open and a large stack of lumber was piled off to one side. A man in a tool belt ducked out, grabbed some of the wood, then walked back through the opening. There were the sounds of men talking and a saw buzzing and the smell that fills the air when wood is cut. It was soothing to him.

Presley pulled him inside, Lulu on their heels, into the space he knew would be her workroom. The man who'd just brought wood inside was setting it down on a pair of saw horses, measuring tape ready to make cuts.

"Hey, Presley," he said. "Seth's got one of the windows framed out front if you want to take a look at it." He looked at the dog. "There are sharp things on the floor. Nails and shit."

James tensed. "She stays with me."

The man shrugged a response but didn't object. James made a mental note to get some kind of boots or something to protect Lu's feet.

"This is James Lawless," Presley said. "James, this is Seb Hart. He and his brothers sold me the building. They do construction around town and also own a bunch of properties in the area."

Seb stopped to shake James's hand. If he thought anything of the fact that James was the failed soldier who had gotten himself captured and tortured, he didn't say anything. He just shook his hand with a nod and went back to work.

Presley turned to James. "This is the workroom," she said and then led him out the door into a tight hallway and gestured at a small door across the hall. "Storage in here."

James poked his head into the room she'd indicated. He would put shelves in here for her. Not the kind made with his split logs. These ones would be functional, either of wood or maybe the wire kind. He'd have to take measurements and see which ones she preferred. He'd also see what she needed to store in there. Depending on her needs, he could make her something custom.

She led the way out toward the store, pointing to a room next to the storage room. "Bathroom," she said. "There's only one, but I won't have a lot of customers in all at once, so it should be fine. They had to open up the doorway to meet the current access requirements, and I'm going to put in all new fixtures."

He stuck his head in and saw a toilet that had seen a lot better days. Even by his standards, which were admittedly low, it wasn't pleasant. Of course, he'd lived in a cell that had a hole dug in the ground for him to piss in during most of his captivity, so he wasn't one to worry too much about rust stains on the porcelain.

And then they walked out into the retail space and she grinned so wide, it took his breath away. He'd never in a million years get tired of the sight of Presley Royale happy.

Two men turned to look over their shoulders and Presley introduced them as two of the other Hart brothers, Shaw and Seth.

He was guessing their mom and dad liked names that started with S.

"Almost done with this one, Pres. Go on outside and take a look," the one named Seth said. Seth was the one Presley mentioned the most, and James found himself assessing the man. He was smart enough to recognize the guy had a look that was attractive to women. He was strong and had dark hair and that stubble that guys in underwear ads all seemed to have.

One of the guys in James's unit had always been obsessed with shaving his stubble down to the point it was short, but not gone all together. The idiot would rub his hand over his chin and say his stubble got him all the girls.

"I'd shake your hand," Seth said, not finishing the thought as he and his brother lifted the window into the frame.

James watched as Presley appeared on the other side of the window, smiling wide and bouncing up and down. "I think she likes it," he said, grinning as the men laughed.

She came running back in and the swell of pride he felt when she jumped right to him and into his arms was probably a little ridiculous. Still, he wrapped his arms around her waist and breathed deep. He was off the ranch, interacting with other people, and he was okay.

She went around, showing him where she wanted to put the reception desk for checking customers out and where she thought the floating shelves could go.

"Katelyn said she could curate some artists to do small hangings for me so the shop could be part of the town's artist night each month. It might bring people in who wouldn't necessarily buy any flowers just then, but they'd see the shop and might remember it when they need flowers."

He pointed to the far corner. "Over there?"

"That's what I was thinking."

Seth ambled over then, sticking his hand out to shake James's hand now that he was free. Then he gestured at the corner he and Presley were facing. "We could install spot lights you can angle in up there, instead of the recessed lighting we're doing everywhere else."

"Let me see what Katelyn says," Presley answered. "I'm not sure what would be best."

James put his hand on Presley's lower back, feeling the need to lay claim to her in front of Seth. Not that the man had done anything to indicate he was interested in Presley, but who wouldn't be? The Hart brothers would have to be dead not to appreciate her. Or gay.

He eyed the men again, hoping maybe they were gay, but he'd never been very good at reading that kind of thing. What were the chances all of the brothers were gay?

"Do you want to show me what you're thinking for the reception desk and I'll take some measurements? How far did you want it to come out?" He pulled the measuring tape he'd brought out of his pocket and moved toward the back corner on the left side of the room.

Seth followed. "Presley told us about the shelves and table you're making for her. I wanted to see if you had any interest in designing a mantle for us. We're flipping a house nearby and it's a pretty bland rectangle. Anything we can do to add a little hint of uniqueness to it will be a big help. We're planning to cut a few windows into it like we're doing here, but it needs more if we're going to sell it."

James glanced to Presley who was busy looking at the corner where the reception area would go, then back to Seth. "I'm happy to look but I don't know if I can promise to have anything ready on a certain schedule." He flexed his hands, knowing on some level he was opening and closing them, but not conscious enough of the movement to stop it.

Lulu interrupted the motion and he buried his fingers in her thick fur.

Seth didn't seem to notice. "We'll be on a tight schedule, but we can always have a backup ready. If you don't have it finished in time, we can install something store bought and use the one you make on another house."

With that, the man went to help his brother lift the next window into place. Just like that, he'd accepted that James wasn't going to be reliable and that was seemingly okay. He wondered how much Presley had told them about him.

Then again, the whole town was probably talking about him. It wasn't any secret he was here and more than likely, people expected him to be bat shit crazy after being in captivity for so many years.

He looked over at Presley. He had to admit, between her, his sister, and the sessions with Sarah, he was beginning to feel like he might come through this. Probably not with all his sanity intact, and probably not as a completely normal person, but for once, he felt like he might have a future that included more than merely trying to survive.

CHAPTER TWENTY-SEVEN

Presley heard the phone ring before she came fully out of the fog of sleep. James's voice didn't sound sleepy at all when he answered, and she wondered if that was a side effect of having lived in the military, needing to awaken quickly and be ready to handle anything on a moment's notice. Or maybe it came from living so many years in captivity when sleeping heavily meant danger.

He was silent after he said hello, listening to whomever was on the other end of the line. When a minute had passed, he swore softly and sat in the bed, cradling his head in his hands.

"I don't know," he said after a minute of trying to control his breathing. She could hear the deep swallows and gulps of air, not at all like the controlled way she had come to expect of him.

"When?"

Presley sat up, pulling the sheet with her to cover her breasts and laying a hand on James's back.

"Okay." He hit the end call button and turned to her,

burying his head in her lap as she wrapped her arms around him.

Presley didn't speak and neither did he. Whatever the call had been about, it was bad. It was an hour or more that they stayed like that.

He didn't cry, or yell, or speak. He didn't close his eyes. He simply stared at the wall, eyes locked on something she couldn't see.

Her arms and legs ached from holding the position, but she held him anyway, knowing he needed this and willing to give it to him. She didn't know why, really. She just knew she would always give him what he needed. Or try to anyway.

She didn't know her reasons for caring so much for this man, but she suspected it was because he never tried to convince her he was anything other than what he was. He never tried to get her to be something she wasn't, either. Never manipulated her or tried to shape her to meet his needs instead of her own. He took her as she was.

When words did come, his throat was scratchy and thick, and she was reminded of times she'd wanted to cry as a child but had held back the tears. It always left her with a painful lump in her throat that wouldn't go away.

"Will you go to Pennsylvania with me?"

Presley didn't ask when or why or for how long. She didn't need to. If he was asking, he needed her. And if he was willing to go to Pennsylvania, something bad had happened.

"Yes," was all she said.

CHAPTER TWENTY-EIGHT

Special Forces Operations Sergeant Eric "Lars" Larson's funeral was to be held in three days' time in Pennsylvania. James and Presley flew out the following day with Lulu accompanying James as his service animal, then rented a car from the airport to Hunt's apartment where they planned to stay.

"Brother." Hunt's greeting was low and solemn as he clasped James's hand. Even Lulu seemed to sense the somber occasion. She stayed closer to James than usual as though she could tell he needed it.

There were others in the room, and some of them murmured greetings to James. He nodded and held fast to Presley's hand as Hunt led the way to a small guest room.

"Sorry about the space," Hunt said, moving a few boxes that stood by the foot of the bed onto an old desk shoved into a corner of the room.

"It's fine," Presley said.

James put their bags on the bed and turned to Hunt. "We're good. We might crash, if that's okay with you."

Hunt nodded. "Holler if you need anything."

He left, shutting the door behind him. Hunt had been the one to find Lars's body after he'd shot himself. Presley couldn't imagine what that was doing to him. She didn't know him well, but even she could see Hunt seemed to take responsibility for everyone around him.

She laid her hand on James's arm. "If you want to go out and visit with everyone, I understand. I'll be fine here." She'd read that veterans often found solace in being with other groups of veterans. That it was a comfort they couldn't find with civilians.

He shook his head, but didn't say anything.

She sat on the bed next to him and took his hand, pressing it between her two. She knew he wouldn't open up to her. Not right then.

The guys he'd been closest to in all the world had been in the firefight that left him a captive, and Hunt and Lars were all that had been left of that unit. She was sure there must be others he'd served with in whatever was larger than a unit—she didn't know enough to know the terms. She didn't press, though. She wouldn't ask where the others were and whether he would want to see them someday. She had a feeling James was one-of-a-kind, or at least one-of-a-very-few, in today's army.

This wasn't like the Vietnam War when there were many prisoners of war. Today, prisoners of war were rare. This left James in a solitary position even among veterans who had served alongside him. She couldn't hope to understand it.

He kicked off his shoes and she did the same before he pulled her onto the bed. Their lovemaking was silent and achingly slow and sweet. He held her and took her with such need it made her weep, but she turned her head and brushed the tears away before he could see them.

She wanted with all her heart to take away some of the pain this man had been dealt. It was too much. It was all too much for any one person to handle.

James clung to her all weekend, refusing to let her leave his side, even when he joined the other veterans after the ceremony at Lars's home. His widow and children were there. All of the other women who had attended the funeral went to the kitchen, but James kept Presley with him, her hand tightly woven in his as though he needed a lifeline. She didn't know how to be a lifeline. She had no idea how to be what he needed, but she stayed with him and held his hand.

The men told stories and joked, often with crass punch lines that made Presley blush. One guy seemed to think that was funny and set out to make her blush again. He stopped when he caught sight of the stare James gave him.

The guy seemed to focus in on James after that and Presley felt the tension in James when he asked a question.

"You really don't remember anything about that day you were caught? You know almost your whole damned unit was killed that day, right? You don't remember any of that, huh? That's pretty good for you, I guess."

Presley stiffened, the edge to the man's tone making her almost as nervous as the slur in his words. He was drinking something amber in a glass, but she didn't know enough to know if it was whiskey or scotch or something else altogether.

All the other men there were looking at the guy like he was an asshole, too.

"Hammond, knock it the fuck off," Hunt said, before James had said anything.

Presley watched James clench his fist, but Lulu came and pressed her head to his hand, then licked his palm when he opened it. He gestured to her and she crawled up, front paws in his lap so he could hold her.

Hammond, the guy who asked the utterly ridiculous question, was currently being herded to another room by Hunt and one of the other guys. He looked like he was trying to focus on what they were saying, like he couldn't understand why what he'd said was so bad.

Later, Presley, James, and Hunt went back to Hunt's place and Presley went to the guest room to change and lay down with Lulu while Hunt and James stayed in the living room. She had a feeling James needed the time with Hunt, without anyone else around and she wanted to give them privacy. James had opened up to her a little over the past weeks, but she knew he might talk to Hunt in ways he couldn't with her.

She could hear the soft sound of the men talking as she curled on her side with Lulu by her feet.

"Sorry, Hammond's an asshole when he gets drunk." Hunt seemed to give the statement some thought, then laughed. "Hell, he's an asshole all the damned time."

"It's all right. Shit, it's not like I don't wonder what the hell happened that day."

"You don't remember any of it?" Hunt asked.

Presley could almost picture the way James would be rubbing the top of his head just then. She wasn't sure he even knew he did it, but he did it anytime he was talking about the memories.

"Bits and pieces are coming back to me." There was a heavy pause, and then, "Do you ever think there was anything off that day? Anything that wasn't like it should have been?"

"I've thought through that day so many fucking times, trying to figure out what the hell went wrong, why it all went ass-pear-shaped so fucking fast." Presley had gotten used to Hunt's swearing. In fact, she noticed, James swore more around these guys, like they somehow gave him permission to do it in some unspoken way.

James didn't answer, but Hunt pressed him. "Why are you asking, Lawless? What do you remember?"

"I don't know. Sometimes I think I'm just losing my mind. Other times, I know there's something I should be remembering about that day. Something I saw that didn't fit. It's like it's right there, but I can't hold onto it long enough to see what it is."

"Let it go, man. It wasn't a day that's worth seeing again, that's for damned sure. We lost too damned much that day."

James murmured a response, but Presley didn't hear it.

"I never understood why you didn't get out when you escaped," Hunt said, and Presley knew what he was referring to, although to be honest, she'd never known for sure if it was just a story or the truth.

Laura had told her there were rumors James escaped his captors at one point, but rather than getting to help to get himself out of there, he stayed in the area and fed information out to the government factions the United States was allied with. The government factions that were trying to fight the violent guerrilla groups and cartels warring for control in the area.

"I was going to run," James said. His voice was low, and now, Presley strained to hear him. Before, she'd been almost trying not to eavesdrop, even though the effort was hopeless. The apartment was so small, there was no way not to hear. "I needed to get to Catalina and bring her out with me. I waited for the sun to go down so I could get to her and her grandmother and get them out of there."

"Catalina?" Hunt asked and Presley was surprised to realize James hadn't told Hunt who she was.

James ignored the question. "Silva killed her. Slaughtered her in front of her grandmother and told her it was payback. I ran, so he killed Catalina."

"You loved her?" Hunt asked.

Again, James didn't answer, but Presley knew the answer.

Instead, he kept talking. "I stayed to kill them all. To kill all the fucking bastards that had hurt her."

And instead, he'd gotten captured again, eventually. It had taken time and he'd fed a lot of intel out to the government in the meantime. But in the end, he'd lost his freedom again because he'd stayed to avenge the woman he loved.

Presley closed her eyes against the injustice of it. James Lawless deserved a break. He didn't deserve the relentless hell life kept piling on top of him.

"But you're out of there now. You have Presley. You have a chance at happiness now. Forget about Silva and all that shit."

The next words out of James's mouth broke Presley's heart.

"Sometimes I think everyone would be better off if I just disappeared. I hurt everyone around me. I don't want that for Presley. She doesn't deserve that."

"You ever think maybe Presley would be hurt more if you left?"

Presley wanted to cheer at Hunt's suggestion. He was right. She realized then how much it would hurt if she lost James. She wanted him in her life. She wanted so much more with him.

James didn't answer the question, but Hunt didn't seem to let that stop him.

"You should ask her if she'd be better off without you. You like to take the choice away from people, sometimes, but I'll tell you, James, I can't handle losing you, too. Not after Lars. I'll go on record right now. I won't be better without you. And if you give Presley the choice, I bet she'd say the same thing. I've seen the way she looks at you and I've seen the way you look at her."

Presley closed her eyes against the pain Hunt's words brought. Even thinking about her life without James hurt.

CHAPTER TWENTY-NINE

James drove in silence the following morning as they worked their way back to the airport. He was surprised it wasn't harder, being out on the road. Other than the visits with Sarah and the one trip to Presley's flower shop, he hadn't left the ranch at all. Lulu lay in the back seat and Presley dozed next to him. When he'd come to bed after talking to Hunt the night before, he'd needed her so much he thought he might burn up with it. He'd woken her again and again in the night, taking her so many times, he thought for sure she'd turn him away. She never did. Her sleepy eyes greeted him with heat and need of their own and he'd let himself go, losing himself in her soft caresses.

The drive to the airport should have been an hour but he was taking them on some back roads that would draw it out closer to two. Traffic made him edgier than fuck, he'd discovered, and he wanted to try to keep himself as calm as possible before having to face the airport crowds and the tight confines of the flight.

They'd rented an SUV and he had the road to himself

at the early hour. He turned the radio on low, watching Presley to see if she stirred at the sound. She didn't bat an eye. Damn, he was really going to have to let her catch up on her sleep when they got home.

He saw the car coming up behind them long before it got to them, but the speed it was traveling closed the distance on them fast. And then it whipped around into the lane beside him on the long stretch of near-empty road.

James was slow to react when he saw the gun. Thought he was having a flashback or imagining shit that wasn't there. Lord knew he did that often enough to expect it now.

Two men, one driving, the other pointing a gun right at James. James swerved and floored it, but the shot cracked out through the silence, waking Presley. James reacted without thought, pushing her down in her seat.

"Unbuckle and get on the floor," he shouted as he swerved toward the car. More shots came and he felt a punch to his arm that he knew damned well meant a bullet had found its mark.

Presley was covering her head with her arms while Lulu stood in the back seat growling and barking like she thought she could fight off the bullets herself.

"Down, Lu!" he shouted as he tried to keep track of where the other car was and what was up ahead of them. She didn't listen and he prayed like hell she didn't get hit by one of the bullets.

Then the car was pulling up beside them again and he was enraged, the anger taking over where the fear had been, turning cold dread to burning heat in an instant. No way in hell was he letting anyone hurt Presley.

James saw the bridge ahead. He kept his foot glued to the floorboard, tearing up the road, trying to keep the man from getting up alongside of them. He didn't want them to be able to get a clear shot. He didn't know what the hell was going on or what these guys wanted, but if they killed him or even just incapacitated him, the SUV might crash and hurt Presley. Or worse, these men might get their hands on her. She would be defenseless.

He had checked his firearm when they flew to Pennsylvania, declaring it and following the requirements of placing it into a hard-sided locked case. It was currently packed into that hard case in his suitcase in the back. He'd thought it was only a crutch to help him feel safer in the outside world.

As they hit the bridge, he lifted his foot off the gas and hit the brakes, then cut the wheel to the left. There was a split second where their attacker's gun was lined up with an open shot into his window, but then the SUV crashed into the sedan and he didn't let up on the pressure as he ducked and felt, more than heard, a bullet hit the headrest behind him.

The scream of the metal guardrail drowned out Presley's cries as he held fast and prayed. They didn't go over the side of the bridge. The guardrail was strong enough to hold. But if he held up the pressure, he could force them over the edge of the road at the other side.

He felt the moment their car went over and he struggled to hold the wheel of the SUV steady so they wouldn't go with their attackers.

The silence that filled the car as he got control of it was thick.

He thought for a brief second about turning back, getting his gun out and making the men eat it as he found out why the hell they'd come after him and who had sent them. One look at Presley and he knew he couldn't risk it.

He'd destroyed everyone who ever got close to him. He'd failed everyone he loved, let them all down. What he needed to do now was get Presley to safety and then get as far away from her as he could.

CHAPTER THIRTY

Neither of them spoke as he drove them away. He didn't head toward the airport. The chances of someone waiting there for them were too great.

James pulled over and checked his arm. He was bleeding but he'd only been grazed. He ignored the wound and pulled back onto the road.

He didn't know for sure, but if he had to place a bet he would put his money on this having to do with the battle that played at the fringes of his memory. Something had happened that night and he needed to find out what.

Disappointment gnawed at his gut as he realized he'd just told Hunt he was remembering bits and pieces of that firefight and within hours someone had tried to kill him. To silence him.

"Where are you going?" Presley asked, and the terror in her voice sent another spiral of self-loathing through him.

"We're going to go to an ATM and take out as much cash as we can." He pulled the car over and pulled out his phone, shutting it off before putting his hand out for hers.

She hesitated. "Shouldn't we call the police?"

"Give me your phone, Pres," he said, not answering her right away. She slipped the phone into his hands and he shut it down, then turned to look at her, hating the fear in her eyes.

He hated worse that he saw trust in her eyes. She might have questioned him a minute ago, but he could see in her face, she believed he could get her through this.

Fuck, he hated that. He was the last person she needed in her world.

"We're not getting on a plane and we can't call the police." Part of him wondered if he wasn't doing the wrong thing. If maybe she was right and they needed to call the police and let them handle this. If he should turn Presley over to them and let someone else keep her safe.

But how could he do that? He might not have memories of the night his life changed forever, but he had a gut sense about it. His gut was screaming that the person behind whatever had happened that night was powerful. It was possible Hunt was involved, but if he was, he wasn't acting alone. It was someone bigger. And James didn't trust that person not to have connections inside police departments.

He didn't trust Presley's safety to anyone but himself.

He sucked in a breath and threaded his hand through her hair, knowing that soon, he wouldn't have the right to touch her like that anymore. That he'd need to walk away and leave her. "They were after me, Presley, not you." They might not have even seen her in the car since he'd gotten her down and she'd been smart enough to stay down.

"What do they want?" Her voice shook when she asked the question and he saw the signs clear as day. Tears filled her eyes. She was cracking.

He needed her to hold on long enough for her to get to safety. He tightened his hold, squeezing her neck a little.

"I'm going to get you home safely, I promise you that. But we can't fly. We need to stay under their radar. Can you trust me to get you home?"

She nodded, tears coming faster now and he hated himself for this, hated that he'd done this to her. He'd brought hell to her doorstep.

Now he needed to draw it away.

They ditched the car and he made sure she understood they couldn't make calls or use her credit cards or anything else that might lead someone to them. He got them to a Greyhound depot and bought tickets home, a trip that would now take them three days instead of hours.

She was quiet for most of the time, only asking once or twice what the men had wanted before she must have realized he didn't have answers.

She was shaking when they got on the bus and he tucked her by his side as Lulu curled into the space at their feet, trained to lay quietly in cramped spaces, when needed.

As Presley slept in his arms for the first leg of the trip, he took advantage, burying his nose in her hair and letting the scent of her seep into him. He wanted to imprint the feel of her, the smell of her, even her taste, onto his senses so he wouldn't forget this. He needed to find a way to keep a part of her with him because he wouldn't be able to bring her with him when he left.

By now, Laura and Cade and probably Presley's parents would be losing their minds with worry. They expected the two of them home earlier in the day and a call to the airline would confirm that James and Presley hadn't made it to the plane. If the SUV was discovered, the police might alert Presley's family that a car she'd rented had been found with bullet holes in the side and evidence of an accident along the length of it.

He knew it was likely the men in the sedan had survived the crash. The edge he'd sent them over hadn't been more than a short drop down to the riverbank below. But by the looks of them, they were former military. If they didn't haul ass out of there before the cops arrived, they would keep their mouths shut.

James closed his own eyes and focused on the flashes of memories he'd been collecting in his journal. He knew he'd seen crates of guns being moved that day. That was out of place. There was no reason he should have seen that.

His unit had been sent into the region to gather intel. It wasn't supposed to go the way it had. They were there to confirm the presence of a cartel leader who had slipped through the hands of the military too many times to count. They wanted eyes on the man before they sent in a drone to take him out.

Of course, he'd been told all that by Hunt when he got back. Whatever information he'd had going into that mission had been locked up in some vault in his brain he didn't have access to.

He opened his eyes again, not wanting to fall asleep until they were further away from the guys with the guns. His gaze landed on a booted foot sticking partially out into the aisle in front of them.

The sight of booted feet tickled his brain again and he knew there was something there. Some connection.

Memory flashed, a voice. The sight of boots on concrete floors. "What the fuck?" Gunshots.

He could hear the voice. "What the fuck?"

Then an answering. "You set this up!" This one from Silva. He'd know that voice anywhere.

Presley stirred in his arms, sitting up and looking out the window. "Where are we?" She asked, pulling her hair free of the ponytail she'd put it in, only to straighten the strands and trap them back in the tie once more.

"I think we passed Springfield about half an hour back." They were traveling through Missouri.

Lulu looked up at him, and he patted his lap, letting her stretch her front paws up onto him. "She needs to get out at the next stop and walk around a bit."

Presley nodded and stood. "I'm going to use the bathroom."

He was numb when he nodded to her. He wanted to keep her next to him. The thought of her so much as walking to the back of the bus to pee was more than he could handle at the moment, but he knew he was going to have to put a lot more distance between them as soon as he got her home to Evers.

He was torn between going to see Hunt so he could confront him and find out what the hell was going on and just heading straight for Washington, DC. Not that he knew what he'd do when he got there.

He thought of General Brophy. He'd been a large part of the push to get James out of South America. But what could he do? Knock on the door of the Pentagon and tell the General he had memories of something bad that shouldn't have happened but did? That he had no idea who the memories were connected to or what they meant, but that he thought they were now putting him in danger? Oh and the one buddy who was alive from that night might be the guy who had sent people after him?

He'd told Hunt he was having memories of the firefight, and the next day, he was shot at and damned near driven off the road.

The whole thing was so fucked up, he didn't know what to do. Maybe he just needed to vanish. There were sure as hell enough veterans living on the streets, he could slip into their ranks and disappear, and no one would need to think about him again.

Presley's hand on his shoulder, made him jump, but she smiled down at him when he turned. Not the bright smile that he'd come to love. This was small and a little sad.

He pulled her down beside him, just wanting to keep her close a little longer.

"Tell me what's going on," she said quietly.

There were murmured conversations taking place all over the bus, but it was nighttime now and the driver had lowered the lights. Most of the people around them were asleep.

"I don't know for sure," he said. "I think it has something to do with my memories. I think maybe I'm not supposed to remember what happened that night."

She raised a hand to cup his face, eyes burning into him. He had to look away. "What will you do?"

"I don't know. There might be a guy who can help me. I have to think about it." He didn't mention that the man who might be able to help was General Brophy. She would likely know the General was Phoebe's father, but he didn't want her involved in this any more than she had to be. He pulled her in, tucking her head to his shoulder. He would deal with this. "Get some sleep."

CHAPTER THIRTY-ONE

James drove for three days after he got Presley home, stopping only for a few hours at a time to sleep on the way to Hunt's place, and watching the building for any sign of Hunt coming or going. He watched for a few hours, but didn't spot him.

It was easy to slip into the building. He simply waited and followed a pair of high school girls who were more interested in giggling and talking than in who was holding the door for them and walking in behind them.

James raised his fist and banged on the door. He and Hunt were now the only two people who'd walked into that firefight and walked out alive. Whatever the hell was going on here, he was going to finish it. Because he'd come to realize something. He wanted what Presley, Laura, and Cade had all been offering him. He wanted a life with family and people he loved around him. He wanted that with Presley. She deserved that kind of life, and he wanted to be the one to give it to her.

His heart tightened at the thought of never seeing her

again. He'd had a life, for just a short frigging time, he'd had people who loved him.

He remembered the day Laura and Cade had come to see him in the hospital. He'd already been out of South America for three weeks by then, but his family hadn't been able to come to him. The military had him under tight security from the start. He could see on her face, she'd wanted to find her brother in that hospital bed. He hadn't had the heart to tell her, her brother was long dead and gone. In his place was an empty shell who couldn't love her the way she wanted him to.

But he was starting to think that the man who'd come out of that jungle might be worth loving. Maybe they would love him as much as Laura had once loved the younger James?

Hunt opened the door, eyes wide when he saw James standing there. Could be because he thought James would be dead. Or it could just be because he thought James would be back in Texas.

"Can we talk?" James asked and tilted his head to indicate Hunt should follow him out into the hallway. He wanted the conversation to take place outside of Hunt's space. He was probably being paranoid, but he didn't trust that someone wouldn't be listening into any conversation that happened in there.

James led the way out to his rental car and slid into the seat while Hunt went to the passenger seat. He didn't tell Hunt he had a gun. He hoped like hell he wouldn't need to use it.

"What's going on, James?" Hunt asked the question like he was talking to a wild animal. Like he thought James had lost his mind and Hunt would need to talk him down.

James didn't blame him, but then again, he didn't

exactly trust him right then. It killed him to think Hunt might have been involved in whatever the hell was going on. Still, he couldn't help but think that Hunt had tried to convince James not to bother trying to remember the fire-fight in the Devil's Den. Did Hunt want James to forget for James's sake or for some other reason?

"You tell me, Hunt. Presley and I didn't get an hour away from your place the other day when we ended up with two men shooting at us."

Hunt's eyes went wide. "What the fuck? Is Presley okay?"

It bothered James that Hunt would even ask about Presley. He growled a response, then grabbed Hunt by the front of his shirt and pulled him toward him in the small space of the car.

"Tell me how they would know where we were going. Tell me how someone might know I was having memories of that firefight."

Hunt opened his mouth to say something, shaking his head like he meant to deny it, then paled. "Oh shit."

James dropped his shirt. "Want to tell me what 'oh shit' means?"

James needed Hunt to be innocent in this. He needed to know this man hadn't betrayed him.

Hunt rubbed his forehead. "I called Gray."

"Colonel Gray?"

"Yeah. I called to see if they could get you more support, get someone who could talk to you. I was worried about the flashbacks and Gray had been supportive the whole time you were missing. He couldn't get anyone to go into the region, they kept telling him it was too unstable, but he stayed in touch with me. He kept trying to get you out, so I thought he could help with what you were going through."

James didn't want to think about the "instability" of the region. He'd seen it firsthand. But if Gray was involved, he could have told Hunt he was trying to get James out, without making any real effort. Instability was definitely an easy excuse, given the state of the area. There was a reason they called it the Devil's Den.

The first fucker who'd had James when he was captured was a cartel drug lord. He was a crazy fucker who had recognized that holding a U.S. serviceman could have its advantages someday. James was a chip to him, something to keep in his back pocket that he might pull out when he was at the bargaining table. In the meantime, though, he hadn't hesitated to torture James. It had been fun to watch the American sweat, to see if they could make him scream.

The man used to talk about making James cry and curl into a ball, to beg for his mommy. They never knew James had done just that on the inside, putting on a mask for the men, but breaking on the inside in ways they would never see.

Peña was the man's name and he was a sick fuck, but that had worked in James's favor for a time. The man had wanted James good and healthy when he tortured him. He'd sent James to Catalina right from the start, to have her heal him. And from time to time, he brought Catalina to James, whenever he thought James might die. He brought her in to bring back his strength. She would weep for James, but he would tell her not to weep. When he was close to breaking, Peña let him see his angel. Catalina was heaven on earth. She was James's reward for hanging on through all they threw at him.

Peña's own cousin killed him. It was a shakeup in the order of things and Peña's cousin had inherited James along with the house and cars and the whole damned thing.

He hadn't been with Peña's cousin long when Silva had taken him. He didn't know if it was payment or what. Peña and his cousin ran the drug cartel, but Silva led an army of rebels and controlled the region. He had dreams of running the whole country someday. James had been in Silva's compound for most of the time he was in captivity. Silva didn't bother with torture. He was happy to let James sit in a cell and starve on rations meant to weaken him and keep him controllable.

James escaped Silva's guards one night, sure he could get to Catalina and get her and her grandmother out of there. He thought he could get them to safety, then he'd either find a way to get them all to the U.S. or he'd just stay there with her, settle someplace and live in peace.

Silva had known exactly how to strike at James. The man had thought nothing of slaughtering Catalina in her home, in front of her grandmother.

James shook off the memories. He'd spent the next year feeding information out, chipping away at Silva's army. Looking for a way to get to Silva himself to kill him. He'd earned the moniker of The Illusion for the way he could blend in and take out men before they realized he was among them.

In the end, though, Silva had been the one to get James when they'd recaptured him.

James forced the memories to sit and wait while he focused on Hunt and Gray. "What did Gray say?"

"He asked if you were still at my place and I told him you were on the road already, headed to the airport. Hell, I even told him you had to leave early since you'd need to take the back roads. He said he'd reach out to you when you got home. That he'd make sure you got help."

"Is Presley okay?" Hunt asked again, quietly this time.

James nodded. "I got her back home."

"What now?" Hunt asked.

James looked at him. "We finish whatever the hell we started when we wandered into that warehouse in the Devil's Den."

CHAPTER THIRTY-TWO

Presley had been home for four days. James had been gone just as long. He'd dropped her off and left again. This time, without her.

Cade was angry, Laura was hurting, and Presley... well, she was trying to hide how much pain she was in. She was beginning to acknowledge to herself, though, that she had stupidly fallen in love with James Lawless. Even being shot at hadn't changed how she felt about him.

She walked into the barn, stopping to greet each of the horses and ponies on her way to Tess's stall. When she got to Tess, the large horse ducked her head and tucked, nuzzling her face in Presley's chest. Presley wrapped her arms around the horse and closed her eyes, trying not to cry. She'd done a lot of crying since coming back from the funeral.

First, she'd cried out of sheer fear as it began to sink into her that she could have easily been killed in that car. That had been before she'd realized James was gone. He'd left sometime in the middle of the night, while she slept in his bed. When she woke, his clothes, his journal, and Lulu were all gone.

He hadn't left a note.

That part probably hurt the most.

She heard Laura's light footsteps as she entered the barn behind her. Presley stood and turned, knowing what her friend would ask.

"Have you heard anything?"

Presley shook her head. "Nothing."

She knew she wouldn't hear anything but she didn't tell Laura that. Laura had thought James was dead for years before they'd discovered he was being held in South America. She'd only just gotten him back and now he was gone again. Presley understood that Laura needed to believe he would return to her again someday.

Presley knew better, though. If he was in danger because of something he'd seen, he would draw that danger as far from his sister as he could. And that meant drawing it from Presley, too.

She realized with a start, that she would have gone with him in a heartbeat if he'd asked. Never mind the fact that she was getting ready to open a new business, that her life and friends were here. She'd have followed him if that was what he wanted.

It hurt like hell that he hadn't. He'd told her all along that he couldn't give her more than temporary, but still, somehow the pain was shocking in its intensity. Its finality, too.

Everything in Evers had been quiet this week. There'd been no fallout from the incident on the way to the airport. Despite the fact that she'd worried the whole way home that they were being tracked, that someone would come out shooting any minute, they hadn't. Except for the fact that James was gone and that Presley now panicked and pulled over anytime a car came up behind her on the road, it was like the incident never happened.

Laura seemed to flail around for something to talk about. She finally settled on the flower shop. It was what Presley had been burying herself in to avoid facing her feelings.

"How are things with the buildout? Are the Hart brothers on track to be ready for the grand opening?"

"Yes." They had needed to find shelves and a table for the back room, and Presley needed to find a counter for the checkout area, since James was now no longer making all of that for her. He left the shelves he'd completed in the barn and she could have used those, but she didn't want the reminder of him on her walls where she'd have to look at them everyday. Instead, Seth had gone to a fixture supply store and picked out basic white shelves that he and his brothers would mount.

Cade walked in and put his hands on Laura's shoulders, squeezing as he stood behind her. Presley turned back to Tess. She didn't want to look at people in love.

"You planning to ride today, Pres?" He asked. Cade never asked her if she'd heard from James. He was too angry with him for hurting Laura.

"Yeah, I thought I'd take her over some jumps. She needs it." Presley needed it, too. The feeling of flying always made her feel better and Tess was a horse that needed to let loose from time to time. Presley couldn't keep her cooped up.

"I put a new barrel jump out there for you to try. It's not too high, but it's broad and it makes for a nice combination with the boxer."

Presley nodded, pulling Tess's halter off the hook and slipping it over the horse's head. She wanted to tack up and get on board as fast as she could. The sooner she was in the ring and away from everyone, the better.

She heard quiet footsteps as the pair walked away. She led Tess from the stall and put her on the crossties to brush her down and saddle her.

She'd gotten the saddle on and was about to switch out the halter for a bridle when her phone rang.

Cursing her stupid heart for flipping over at the thought it might be James, she pulled it from her pocket. It wasn't James and it wasn't ever going to be James. It was Ashley's husband, Garrett Hensley. Aside from being married to Ashley, Garrett was also Chief of Police for Evers. He'd had to interview her for the Pennsylvania police when her rental car had been found torn up with bullet holes and ditched behind an old barn on the side of the road.

"Hey Garrett," she said, trying to sound normal. If he could tell she'd been crying, he would tell Ashley and then Ashley would run over to check on her again.

"I just got a fax with a copy of the police report for you. You're going to need it to make a claim on your insurance."

Presley grimaced. If ever there was a time to have bought the rental car no-questions-asked insurance policy, this would have been it. She wondered how much it raised your premiums to have your car riddled with bullets. "Okay, thank you."

"Do you want me to drop by with it sometime? Or I can give it to Ashley to get to you."

"No, that's okay. I'm going to go into the flower shop tomorrow to check on a few things. I'll run by the station and pick it up, then, if that's okay."

"You got it, Presley."

He hung up and she had a new appreciation for tough guys who didn't ask questions and didn't want to have touchy-feely conversations about your emotional state.

CHAPTER THIRTY-THREE

Looking at the sign out front of her shop should have filled Presley with all kinds of happy feelings. The logo had come out better than she'd expected, a ring of flowers laced around the name of her shop didn't sound very fancy, but the look and feel was everything she was going for and more. *Petals and Posies*.

She unlocked the door and went inside. The windows had been finished out in the front and the walls were painted and ready to go. Still, nothing was as it should have been. There were plain white shelves on the wall and a granite counter for the check-out area. It lacked all the custom touches that should have made the space perfect.

The Hart brothers would be back the following day when the refrigerated cases were due to arrive. After they installed them, there was little left to be done. Then she'd have a week to set up the computer and get the software up and running. She had to enter inventory into the system and then check in the stock that would arrive for her grand opening.

She moved to the work room, pretending not to notice

the basic sturdy table that filled the space. It was large and functional. And it made her want to cry. She heard the door open at the front of the shop and closed her eyes for a second. It was either one of the girls stopping by after seeing her car out front or one of the Hart brothers checking on things.

Either way, she didn't want to see any of them.

When she saw the large figure filling the doorway to the work room, she didn't process what was happening at first.

She opened her mouth to say that they weren't open for business yet, but something was off about the man. He wasn't smiling. There was no emotion there, only cold, dead eyes looking at her as he moved toward her. Presley opened her mouth to scream, but he was on her, covering her mouth with a hard hand. He pressed his hand into her, making her teeth bite into the soft inside of her mouth.

"You need to keep your mouth shut, do you hear me?"

It wasn't a real question and he didn't wait for an answer. He'd lifted her easily with one arm and was walking her toward the back door. She kicked at him, but there was no way for her to get any leverage and he had her arms locked by her sides. The adrenaline rush that hit her was useless.

When he got to the back door, he leaned in close to her ear. "Keep your mouth shut, you hear me?"

He pulled his hand from her mouth so he could unlock the back door. She screamed, but the sound was cut off when he gripped her hair tight, and cursed as he slammed her head into the doorjamb.

She didn't hear his words, only knew he was cursing her for making noise. She saw another man, and a van. She struggled as they put her into the back of it, her head splitting where he'd knocked it against the door. She thought she felt blood, but the panic rising up in her was taking over everything, making it hard to decipher what was going on.

"Did anyone see you?" one guy asked.

"No." The guy who grabbed her was putting zip ties on her wrists, cutting into her flesh. He did the same to her legs, though those were protected by her jeans. Then he put a cloth bag over her head and her panic flew into the stratosphere as light was blocked out and she realized this was really happening.

CHAPTER THIRTY-FOUR

James and Hunt were two hours away from the Pentagon when he got the call. They were planning to go to General Brophy. He was the one guy James could trust right now. Brophy was loyal to his country, to his family, and to the men who served under him. No way in hell would he be involved in any of this.

The voice on the other end of the phone line was Gray's. And in that moment, James knew it was also the voice he'd remembered in his flashbacks. It was the voice of the man who'd said "What the fuck?" just before Silva's voice had cut in. What Colonel Gray would have been doing in a warehouse with Silva was a mystery, but James had a feeling he knew.

"I've got your girl, Lawless. Presley Royale is going to be staying with me as my guest until I get you."

Ice hit his veins. James would tear the man's head off and enjoy watching the life drain from his body.

He didn't bother telling Gray he would see him dead. He didn't take the time to threaten him and let him know what he'd do to him if Presley was hurt. He said the only thing he could. "Where?"

"Head toward Alexandria. I'll text you an address later."

"I'm four hours out." It was a lie, but he needed the extra time.

"I can be a patient man. But mind you, Lawless, don't fuck around. I'm not that patient. And if I get bored, I'll play with your girl. I don't think you want that."

"You fucker—"

James was talking to a dead line. The man had hung up. The sound of blood rushing in his head was something James had heard often in his life, but it was never more overpowering, more all-consuming than now. He'd left her to protect her, to keep her safe. If she wasn't part of his life, she wouldn't be hurt. He'd been wrong. He'd left her and now they were using her against him.

"What is it?" Hunt asked from beside him.

"Gray has Presley. He's holding her in Alexandria until I turn myself in to him."

"He'll kill you," Hunt said.

"Yeah. And he's probably already sending someone after you. We're the only loose ends in all of this."

James made a U-turn as Hunt punched Alexandria into the rental car's navigation system. He was on his way to end this and get Presley the freedom she deserved. Even if that meant walking into a death trap himself.

CHAPTER THIRTY-FIVE

Presley had cried herself out before they got her to the dirty room. The ride in the van had been long, maybe an hour or more. Her legs and hands had been asleep long before they got her out of it. The sounds of helicopter blades and men yelling over them had been all she heard as she was loaded onto the aircraft.

She could be anywhere now, she realized. They had cut the bindings on her hands and legs but kept her head covered. There had been a car ride after the chopper and then she'd been left in a room. The last man to walk out pulled the cover from her head and ripped the tape from her mouth, tearing at her skin.

The room was nearly empty with only a small cot in the corner where she sat. There was only one door and there wasn't a window anywhere. She'd never felt more terrified, but the sensation was mingled with disbelief. This couldn't be happening. It had to be a nightmare.

She thought of James and how he must have felt in captivity all those years. He must have spent days on end alone. She'd been alone for an hour and she thought she would lose her mind from the sheer terror of it. If her captors didn't come back, there would be no way for her to survive. She would starve to death, with no food and no water. The thought of it made her almost want to laugh, the kind of crazed laugh that came from knowing you might be losing yourself, losing your mind.

She wasn't sure if her captor walked in just then, would she hug the man, out of sheer relief that he hadn't left her?

She thought she might.

How had James handled this for so damned long?

Would he be coming for her? Surely this had to be connected to him. He'd said the men had shot at them because of the memories he was trying to recover. Maybe they'd taken her to force his hand. To get him to come to them?

Or could this be completely unrelated? No. She dismissed the thought. It couldn't be. It had to be connected to James, so he would come, right?

She paced the room, stretching her sore limbs. There was nothing she could do to try to escape. There was nothing in the cell. No door knob on the inside of the door. There was nothing.

Noise outside the door warned her that someone was coming and she stepped back, even at the same time as she realized how useless the gesture was. There was no place for her to go. No way to hide or get away.

The men who entered wore tan pants and lose white shirts that made Presley think they were dressed for a tropical climate. When they spoke in heavy accents, she had the strange sensation that maybe she'd been taken to a foreign country, but that couldn't be, could it? She shook her head. She hadn't been in the helicopter long enough to make it out of the country. Even going to Mexico would have taken longer than they'd been in the air. At least, she thought. In truth, she had no idea how fast a helicopter could travel.

The sensation of being lost and not having any idea where she was or how much time had passed was dizzying.

"Come, Silva waits for you," one of the men said as they took hold of her arms.

Presley froze, fear making her whole body run cold. She dug in her heels, resisting their pull as her mind reeled. It couldn't be Silva. The man responsible for torturing James all those years? He couldn't be here. Couldn't know about her.

Panic clawed at her throat as bile flooded it. This couldn't be happening.

"No," she said, wrenching her arms and trying to flee.

The man who'd spoken, dropped her arm and struck her hard with the back of his hand. She felt the pain of the blow and tasted blood, crying out. Then, they were pulling her again, taking her out of the room. She expected to be in some hidden underground bunker without windows or exits, but she wasn't.

Presley was in large warehouse. She turned and looked over her shoulder, realizing the room she'd been locked in had been a free-standing structure built into the corner of the room. They dragged her from the warehouse only to enter another one, set close by. In a corner of the large space, a small table sat in front of a dark-haired man with a scar down one side of his face.

His smile as she approached was wicked and he stood to greet her as though she were meeting him in a five-star restaurant on a date.

"Ms. Royale, I am Rodrigo Silva, it is such a pleasure to meet you."

She wondered if he was going to offer his hand for her

to shake and the thought made her realize just how much she'd split from the reality of the situation.

"Sit." It was a command. Silva sat in a chair at the table and pointed to a chair on the other side.

It was then she realized he was eating a meal. He didn't speak as he ate. The sight of the food made Presley's stomach cramp, like it wanted to make sure she didn't try to put any food in there right now. Her body was probably in emergency mode, not wanting to deal with the normalcy of processing food or water.

Silva pushed his plate to one side and leaned back in his chair, one hand on his stomach. "We will wait. Your James will come and this will all be finished soon." He spoke in an almost offhand way, as though telling himself more than he was telling her.

"Yes, this will be finished soon."

CHAPTER THIRTY-SIX

James pulled the car over outside of Alexandria. He had lied to Gray. They weren't four hours out. They'd only been two. He pulled into a Walmart parking lot and looked at Hunt.

"I'm okay with you sitting this out. You don't need to do this."

Hunt gave him a hard look. "Like hell I'm letting you walk into this alone."

James hesitated. "We should call General Brophy."

Hunt nodded. "When we get to Presley, we'll give him a call. Let him know. But we don't wait for backup."

"Agreed."

They walked into the store side-by-side. James had his gun, but he needed more than that right now. He needed to transform back into The Illusion if he was going to have any chance of saving Presley.

They made their way to the clothing section. James already had a pair of cargo pants on, but his white t-shirt had to go. The pants were dark navy, so they would do, but he grabbed a long-sleeved dark green shirt. He also grabbed a long-sleeved tan shirt and a pair of khaki cargoes, in case it turned out dressing lighter would help him blend in more. How you needed to dress always depended on your background. Hunt chose similar items.

They made their way to the hunting section next, testing the weight of various blades. James chose two Bowie knives and a skinning blade with a sheath that would attach around his ankle. A rifle scope and a trip to the ammo section for incendiary bullets, and to the camping section for lighter fluid, and he was good to go.

When they got back to the car, they had no choice but to wait for the call from Gray, telling them where to go. James closed his eyes and played the images from his memories again, sifting through them. The crates, the boots, the voice, "What the fuck?"

The voice was the same. He was sure of it. Gray and Silva had both been in the warehouse the day his squad had been ambushed. There had been gunfire then, muffling the voices that followed, but the surprise in those voices was unmistakable.

Again, he played it all. The boots. The guns, the sounds of the crates being stacked. Crate after crate of weapons. The writing on the sides of the crates.

James's eyes shot open. They were U.S. Military markings on the outsides of the crates.

Hunt was looking at him. "You remember more?" Hunt and Lars had been outside the building when all the shit had gone down. They were there to support a drone strike. It should have been an in-and-out mission.

James nodded. "Peña was there, but so were Silva and Gray. Both of them seemed surprised when we hit the building. Gray didn't know we were coming. And there were crates of U.S. guns and ammo."

"You think Gray was selling weapons to Silva?"

"Silva, or Peña." James paused. "Maybe both. I think Silva and Peña cooperated when it was beneficial to them both, but I saw their men invade and attack each other, too. I've always thought Silva had something to do with Peña being killed by his cousin."

Hunt had the same hard look James probably had then. Knowing someone in their military was sending weapons over there for profit was the ultimate betrayal. If those weapons weren't used there on the ground against their own men, they might easily end up in other areas where the U.S. had men and women fighting. The chances those weapons would be used to kill U.S. Military members was high. That, or innocent people who lived in terror in that region.

James sat up as his phone rang. "Yeah?"

The voice on the other end of the line was different this time, at least he thought it was. He couldn't be sure of much anymore, but he didn't think it was Gray.

The man rattled off an address and hung up. That was it.

James plugged the information into the car's GPS and looked at the route mapped out for him.

The place was outside Alexandria, but James didn't recognize the location. He pulled up Google maps and plugged in the address then switched to Google Earth view and saw that he was headed toward warehouses. Open spaces around the warehouses made it hard to slip in and out unnoticed. He would be in open space, making it more than easy for anyone to pick him off as he approached. He had his work cut out for him.

CHAPTER THIRTY-SEVEN

Madman didn't even begin to describe the man sitting across from Presley. Silva had spent the last hour telling her about his country, his love for its beauty and its people. She knew he tortured and killed indiscriminately. But he seemed to see himself as a hero in all of this.

She still didn't understand what he was doing here in the United States. Why would he have come after James here? She suddenly pictured him as this weird little cartoon character like the guy in that moose cartoon with the Russian woman. She had no idea what the name of the cartoon was or why it flashed into her mind, but she thought of Silva now, with a little cartoon version of his pot belly and the slim mustache that seemed almost drawn across his upper lip. And he was boarding a cartoon plane to hunt down his nemesis, the American who wouldn't die no matter what he did to him.

A laugh bubbled up and escaped before she could control it and then she was laughing and there wasn't any stopping it. Her captor eyed her with interest as she waved her hand in front of her face. Heaven help her if he thought she was laughing at him. She couldn't stop herself, though.

God, what was wrong with her? She should be trying to figure out how to get away from this man, not laughing at him. But it was really hopeless, wasn't it? How in the world did she think she could get herself out of this?

The look on Silva's face was shifting from curiosity to annoyance, and seemed to be well on the way to anger when a car pulled into the warehouse. Since the men posted at the entrance of the structure did nothing to stop it, she guessed Silva knew who was coming.

He stood. "You will excuse me, Ms. Royale."

He shouted something in his native language and one of the men in tan and white came to stand with Presley.

Silva went to the car and she watched as a man in a U.S. Military uniform stepped out and looked to where she sat.

Silva opened his arms wide. "You got me all the way here and this is how you treat me? You have me waiting like your dog in a warehouse?"

The other man wasn't the least bit cowed. He was in Silva's face as he answered, almost pushing the man back with how much he invaded his body space. "If you had ended this all years back like I told you to, we wouldn't be in this position. I'm not going to handle this one for you, Silva. I've got your little ghost or whatever the hell you call him coming here, but you need to handle this."

Presley heard the man who'd been sent to guard her whisper a name and she knew it. The Illusion. James was coming, and if the tone of her guard's voice was anything to go by, that fact had the man on edge.

"If you had done your job to begin with, none of this would have happened. You were the big man, you said."

Silva was taunting the man from the military now. He was shoving right back into the man's space. "You told me you knew everything the U.S. Military did in the area, that you could warn me anytime they would be there. Maybe you lied to me? Maybe you set up the attack that day?"

The men fought, arguing over which one of them needed to take care of the loose ends they'd created. The military guy seemed to think Silva should have killed James years before instead of letting Peña keep him. Silva said he would still have James if the guy had kept up his side of the bargain.

Presley took advantage of the moment to see if her guard was watching her. He wasn't. His eyes were on the door to the warehouse, as though he thought someone might come crashing through any minute, guns blazing. She remembered Laura telling her that James had been called The Illusion during the time he escaped from Silva and was feeding information back out to the government and trying to bring Silva down.

He'd been given the name when he targeted Silva's men. The rumors spread with stories of a man who could take down ten or more men before any of them realized there was a threat in their midst. From the way the man watched the door, she would guess he expected The Illusion to come calling tonight, and he wasn't looking forward to the visit.

Presley slid the fork off Silva's discarded dinner plate and slid it up the sleeve of her sweater. Then she pushed his napkin over his plate hoping Silva wouldn't notice the utensil missing. If there was a knife on the table, she'd have taken advantage of that, but there was not.

Maybe he didn't think she had it in her to stab him in

the eye with a fork, but if she got her chance, she would do just that without any hesitation. She knew damned well there was no way he would just let her go when James showed up. Whatever the man had planned, he didn't intend for her or James to walk out of here alive.

CHAPTER THIRTY-EIGHT

James looked through the scope he'd bought, watching for movement. They'd left Lulu in the car, and he hoped like hell he could keep his head in the game without his service dog by his side. It made him glad he'd brought Hunt. It was a damned good thing Hunt hadn't been involved or James would be here without anyone to back him up. Not that the two of them together against who knew how many well-armed men was the best setup, but James had faced worse odds. The sun would be going down soon. He needed to see what he was dealing with before that happened, then wait for cover of darkness to move.

He'd waited once before for darkness to come and had found Catalina dead as a result. Still, he needed it if he was going to survive this. So far, he'd seen one man on the two back corners of the warehouse and at least four men in the opening at the front. He would bet there were more inside.

"Only one man working the perimeter," he said to Hunt, who lay beside him. Still, they had to move quickly. He would bet the men were in radio contact. Once he took one man out, they would figure out he was there quickly.

Not to mention, they expected him to walk in any minute and try to exchange himself for Presley. What would happen if he didn't arrive soon?

James glanced at the sky, which was only beginning to darken. There was still time before the night would truly fall.

He went back to his car and pulled out the khaki pants he'd bought at the store. He pulled off the dark t-shirt and dark pants he'd put on and swapped them out for the khakis and the white t-shirt he'd worn earlier in the day. The men were all wearing tan pants and white shirts. With any luck, they'd let him get closer to them if they thought he was one of them.

It was a uniform James knew well. He looked at Hunt, who wore dark pants and a dark shirt. "Silva's men wore these khaki pants and white shirts on his compound in South America." Hunt's eyes went wide at the news. James didn't know how, but somehow, his nightmare had followed him home.

Silva had made a mistake. When James had been on Silva's turf, he'd been injured or half-starved and weak. James was stronger now. Silva wouldn't walk out of this alive.

"If I'm dressed like them, I might be able to get close enough to take them out quietly. You hang back and pick off anyone you can get to. I'm going to need you to distract them when I go in the front door."

Hunt cursed, but didn't argue. There was no way around this. Hunt had called and left a message for General Brophy at the Pentagon on the way there, but they had no idea when the man would get the message, or if he'd take it seriously.

James couldn't wait any longer. The perimeter

patrolman was on the side of the warehouse. If James had approached him out front or at the back, he would have been exposed. Hunt worked his way to the back of the building while James crept silently toward the man on the perimeter, waiting until he turned away before moving forward. He drew the Bowie knife, sure and steady in his hand, the point facing backward toward his elbow. It might be a new knife, but the sensation was an old one. The soft gurgle as the man's throat filled with blood was one he'd heard before. It was one he hadn't thought he'd have to hear again.

He'd been wrong.

James dropped the man in the dry brush on the outer edge of the airfield, then took the man's weapons, tucking the handgun into his waistband and slinging the semiautomatic assault rifle over his shoulder. There wasn't much more he could do to hide the body. He dropped to the ground and belly crawled, moving slowly away from the area. He would need to back away, then circle to the back and approach again.

The time ticked by as he moved into position. He used the cover of a nearby warehouse to come up close to the position of one of the men at the back, then tossed a rock to draw the man out. It was easy to get people to move where you wanted them to. They wanted to investigate. The man took a few steps in the right direction and James stepped out from the shadows and took him down, using the Bowie again, his appreciation for its swift action as strong as ever.

The only downside to using the Bowie was the blood it spilled on the man's clothes. If he'd taken him without all that, James could have used the man's shirt to better match the uniforms of the guards.

It was no matter. The t-shirt was close enough to the button-down shirts the men wore to fool them.

Hunt moved forward and took the other man out in much the same way, then they collected their weapons and met up at the back of the building. James looked to Hunt, then to a metal drum that sat by the back steps of the loading dock. Probably, it was used to put out cigarettes.

He strapped one of the weapons he'd taken to his back and tossed the others into the barrel. Hunt dug through his duffel for the lighter fluid, passing it to James, then loaded the incendiary bullets into the gun he'd taken from the man he'd knocked out.

James looked at Hunt now, his only backup. "Wait until you see me go in. Give me a twenty-count after that, then light it up."

It wouldn't make a big explosion, but the incendiary bullets would light the lighter fluid and the heat would make the other bullets go off like loud fireworks as their shells expanded and blew apart. It was all the distraction he'd need.

He slipped the long-sleeved shirt over his white top, helping him to blend into the dark a little bit, then backed away again, putting some space between himself and the warehouse as he moved around to the front of the building.

He raised the LR300 he'd taken from one of the men and looked through the scope to the front of the warehouse. It was dark, but Silva's men were stupid. They stood framed in the open doorway with the light of the warehouse behind them, their silhouettes giving him a perfect shot.

He raised it to his target and took down the first man with a single shot. The others were so startled, they turned and stared at the spot where the man had been in an almost comical way. James shot the man on the other side, the one furthest away from his first shot. The two in the center spun to look at the newly felled man.

Two more men appeared from inside the warehouse and James could hear shouts and calls. The crackle from the radio of the perimeter man sounded behind him, from where James had left his body lying. James took out two more of the men with a fully automatic burst as the others ran back inside the warehouse for cover.

And then he saw her. Rodrigo Silva shouted as he pulled Presley into the spotlight of the entranceway.

"Lawless! I find myself in possession of another of your beautiful women. I must tell you, you do have exquisite taste. Ms. Royale is every bit as lovely as your Catalina was."

James stilled, then called out to Silva. "I'll come in if you let her walk away. When I see her walk away, I'll come in. No fighting."

Silva laughed as James knew he would. He was watching, waiting for an opening to take the man out without putting Presley at risk. Or, at least, at too great a risk. It didn't matter how good of a shot he was, she was going to be in some danger of being hit.

"Catalina begged me, you know. She begged for mercy. Told me she wasn't really yours, that you didn't care about her. I knew she was lying. I saw the way you looked at her, saw what she did to you. You were weak because of her, just as your love for Ms. Royale makes you weak now."

James could try to call out, try to convince Silva that he didn't love Presley. That holding her held no sway over him. It wouldn't work, though, and truth be told, he couldn't bring himself to say the words. He loved Presley more than life itself. Hadn't been willing to admit it to himself until now, but it was there. Deep inside of him, his love for her swelled. All he had left in him that was still human, that still had the capacity to love, it was hers.

Then, Presley was moving. She turned and wrenched free. She lashed at Silva with something, shoving once, twice. Silva cried out and clutched at his neck and James took the shot.

Silva fell. Presley seemed frozen in place for long beats of time, then she turned to run.

James began to move toward her, weapon raised, ready to provide cover, but she didn't make it two steps before a man dove out and grabbed her, drawing her back into the warehouse.

James had no shot. There was no way for him to fire without hitting her. There was no way to stop as Colonel Gray grabbed her. And then she was gone, disappearing back into the warehouse.

CHAPTER THIRTY-NINE

James had to move now, and he had to move fast. He didn't know for sure how many people were in that warehouse.

Two of Silva's men had disappeared back into the warehouse when James shot Silva. There could be more of them, but he would bet Silva had sent all of them out the minute the shooting started. On his home territory, Silva would have been in a stronghold, guarded by upwards of a hundred men, but he wouldn't have traveled with so many.

"The only way for you to end this, James, is to come in here and turn yourself over to me!" It was Gray.

James prayed like hell his mind didn't choose now to flashback to South America and shut him down. He needed to stay in the present if he was going to get Presley out of there.

"She's going to die and I'm not going to make it painless for her!"

James ignored the shouting and rounded the back of the warehouse, creeping back up on it with a low whistle to Hunt to let him know he was coming. There was a single entrance point on this side. Just a regular door, not a wide entrance like on the front. Gray didn't have the door covered. He thought James was still up front.

James listened to the shouting of the man inside as he threatened to do unspeakable things to Presley if James didn't come in.

"I'm coming, Presley." He whispered the words under his breath and nodded to Hunt, holding up his hand with all five fingers splayed out in signal. James moved back to the front of the warehouse as he heard Hunt fire at the barrel. Two shots and the barrel went up.

James heard the shouts of the men in the warehouse as they moved toward the sounds of the bullets bursting in the barrel at the back of the space, firing their own weapons toward the sound. He moved, entering through the front and spotting Silva's men at the back. He took them down, then turned to scan the warehouse, keeping himself behind a stack of metal barrels. They didn't provide much cover, but they were all he had. He saw Presley, standing ramrod straight in the center. Behind her stood Gray.

James must be losing his mind. He remembered playing the game CLUE with his sister when they were kids. *I think it's Colonel Mustard in the library with the wrench.*

Only this was Colonel Gray in the warehouse with the gun.

James laughed. "You know, the funny thing about all of this, Colonel, is that I still don't fucking remember a damned thing from that night. My head's so fucked up, those memories will probably never come out." It wasn't entirely the truth. He didn't remember enough, though, to testify against the colonel. If the man hadn't grabbed Presley, James probably wouldn't have been able to give the military much to take Gray down.

Gray rarely entered the field anymore, but he knew

enough to have himself behind Presley and the gun wedged at her side.

"You're a loose end I can't afford, Lawless. Why the hell you didn't die years ago, I'll never understand. Silva was like that, though. Always thought he knew better than anyone. Thought he was untouchable."

James watched, waiting for the man to let his guard down, to move his weapon or forget to hold so tight to Presley that James might get a shot in.

He could see Hunt entering the warehouse through the back door.

Presley's face was white as hell as James watched. He knew she had to be terrified. He'd brought this down on her. He'd done this. But he would get her out of there.

"Doesn't matter. It was time for me to retire, but I'm not going to look over my shoulder all my life wondering if you might start to remember something." The colonel sounded tired now, like he was feeling sorry for himself.

"I'll offer you the same deal I offered Silva. Let Presley walk out of here and I let you walk away," James said. "Same as Silva," he repeated looking at Presley as he said those last words, hoping Presley might pick up on the message. If she could move like she did with Silva, maybe James could get a shot in.

Far away in the distance, the sound of sirens started, and the colonel looked to the opening in the warehouse.

"Did I forget to mention I called General Brophy? That'll be him." That or someone had called the police when they heard the gunshots. Either way, James wanted Gray to realize Brophy knew what he'd done. "Same as Silva."

Presley moved, wrenching and shoving while Gray was distracted by the sirens. Gray's gun went off, but Presley was moving and James came out from behind the barrels, one shot, two. Gray was down and Presley was running to the door.

Hunt was coming up behind Gray, ready.

James walked toward Gray. The man was down, but he raised his gun.

James fired at the same time Hunt did.

CHAPTER FORTY

The bullet hit James as he watched Gray go down.

James wanted to go to Presley to see that she was okay, but his knees buckled, and he fell to the ground.

He heard Presley, then felt her hands on him. Hunt was by his other side.

"James, there's an ambulance coming. Hold on James, hold on." Hunt was talking to him, but had his phone in his hands.

Presley's hands were on him and he could see tears streaking her cheeks. James wanted to tell Presley to run, that she needed to be safe. That was all he needed, for Presley to be safe. He could hear the police entering, Presley and Hunt trying to explain to them that they needed to let the EMTs help James. That he wasn't the bad guy.

He heard Brophy's voice, the deep booming command in it that marked him as a General more than his uniform ever could.

James closed his eyes. Presley was safe. The police were there. She would go home to the ranch and start her flower shop and live a life away from him. Away from all the fucked-up shit that followed him.

James felt it when they rolled him onto the backboard. He felt them lift him to the ambulance. He didn't want to feel any of it. He wanted to float away and be done with everything.

CHAPTER FORTY-ONE

James woke suddenly, the urge to get to Presley over-whelming him. Then she was there, pushing at him, trying to get him to lay down. He recognized the smells of the hospital.

Strong hands added to Presley's and pushed him down and there were voices around him. Some he recognized, other he didn't.

Cade and Laura were there, but all James cared about was Presley.

"Are you okay, Pres?"

She moved into his line of sight and smiled at him. "I'm fine, but you need to stay down." She glanced over to his side where he heard a machine beeping. He didn't care.

James closed his eyes. "I'm so sorry. I never thought they'd grab you. I didn't even think they'd seen you in the car."

"They didn't," Cade said. "General Brophy said Gray tracked who you flew to Pennsylvania with and saw the rental car his men shot up was in her name. He probably figured there was a chance you were at least close friends, if not more."

"We're more," James said, his eyes on Presley's face. "So much more." Now he was talking only to her.

"Let's give them some privacy," Laura said and he waited while Cade and Laura left the room.

"I was so scared," Presley said, holding his hand with both of hers.

James couldn't move his left arm but he lifted his right hand from hers and cupped her cheek. "I'm so sorry they scared you. I'd do anything to take that away."

"I thought they were going to kill you. After all you've been through, when Silva told me who he was, I thought he was going to kill you."

"Is Silva dead?" He'd seen him go down, but the man could have survived. For that matter, Gray could still be alive.

"They're both dead. They took Hunt in custody at the scene but the General was there and said he'd get it sorted out. They have a guard on your door, as though they thought you might get up and walk away."

The mention of being confined to a room, even a hospital room, set James on edge immediately.

Presley squeezed his good hand, and he knew she'd understood right where his head had gone. "I'm working on getting permission from the hospital administrators to get Lulu in here for you."

"How about we get me out of here instead?" He tried to lighten the tone, but the effort failed. There was no mistaking the panic in his words.

"The General is working on it and Cade's brother got you a lawyer who has experience with military courts."

"I couldn't wait for them to get you out of there. I didn't

know if the General would be able to act quickly enough or what Silva might do if I didn't show up. He'd already killed one woman I loved. I couldn't let him take you from me, too. It would have killed me."

A doctor came in then, interrupting them before he could tell Presley everything he was feeling. And then she was gone, pushed out by one of the nurses who'd entered with the doctor. James didn't listen as they talked to him about the surgery he'd need on his arm. They were going to try to piece him together, but he didn't care. He wanted to talk to Presley, to make sure she knew he didn't want this to be casual anymore. He wanted so much more than that with her.

CHAPTER FORTY-TWO

Presley was shaken as she left the room. Laura and Cade were there, and Laura wrapped her arms around Presley. The contact helped, but her emotions were so all over the map, she didn't know how she'd ever feel normal again. First, she'd been through the sheer terror of the kidnapping, then she watched as Silva was shot and she'd gone through the infinitesimally small moment of feeling like she was free. When Colonel Gray had grabbed her, she'd almost shut down completely. Then James had been there. He was there, and he'd gotten her through it. But when she saw the bullet hit him, saw him go down, her fear went to all new levels.

Fear and anger at what Silva and Gray had put James though. He'd been through so damned much and he didn't deserve any of it.

Waiting for him to wake up in that room was agony. She wanted to whisk him away, to get him back to the safety of his loft in the barn, tucked away on the ranch. She wanted this to be over, to know they were safe and he was going to heal. From the arm injury, but also from everything else that had happened to him.

She hadn't missed his words in there. He'd talked about his feelings for her and for Catalina as though they were one and the same, but she wouldn't get her hopes up that he meant to say he loved her. She'd gotten her hopes up in the past when she read too much into what a man told her.

"He's going to be okay, Presley. We'll bring him home and he'll be better now." Laura's words ended on a sob and Cade pulled his wife into his arms.

Presley wrapped her arms around herself now, listening as Laura cried, but she didn't cry herself. She knew if she let the tears come, they wouldn't stop.

It was so damned unfair to see this man go through anything else. It was too much. The fear that it would break him was too great. What if he never made it back from this?

Presley looked up to see two figures coming down the hall and her breath caught.

General Brophy and Hunt were coming toward her.

"How is he?" the General asked when they got to her.

"He's in with the doctor now. They need to operate on his arm," Presley said. She had heard the doctor talking about the physical therapy James would need to go through after the surgery. She knew this meant he wouldn't be able to do the wood working that had been helping him cope with his PTSD. One more thing that had been taken from him, but she could hope this was only temporary. The doctor had sounded like he'd get back the majority of function in that arm.

She looked at Hunt and then at the General. "Did they make any decisions about bringing Hunt and James up on charges?"

The General gave a small nod. "They were acting under my authority. There won't be any fallout for them."

She wondered if that meant there'd be fallout for him. Or maybe it was just that there'd be fallout for other people in the Pentagon who hadn't realized Gray was selling arms and ammunition to a South American guerrilla leader all this time.

As if in answer to her question, the General spoke. "He was working with one of the contractors that makes weapons for the armed forces. For years, they've added small amounts of extra weapons and ammunition to orders that Gray had siphoned off and stored, then he'd deliver them to Silva. Silva kept some, but others were sold to drug cartels in the area, and some went overseas to quasi-political entities.

"So, it's over?" Laura said, coming up beside them.

Presley held her breath.

The General nodded. "It's over. We'll get him through surgery, and get him home."

Presley's hands shook as she watched the doctor and nurses leave the room. She watched as the General went in to talk to James.

When the others had all left, she went in to him. He watched her quietly from the bed.

"When will they take you to surgery?" She asked.

"Another hour."

She stood a few feet from the bed, not sure what to say to him. She didn't really know what her place was in his world.

"Come here, Pres." He reached for her and she went to him, feeling a little like she was hanging in a void, waiting for her world to right itself.

And then he righted it for her. "I love you. I was afraid

to say it before because I don't deserve you, Presley. I should have pushed you away a long time ago because I don't think I'll ever be normal. I think I'll be half fucked up in the head for the rest of my life. But if you'll have me, I'm going to be completely selfish and do what will make me happy instead of what I think is right this time. I can't help it, because I'm not strong enough to give you up."

In that instant, Presley could breathe again. She'd always felt just a little off all her life. She'd known she wasn't like most kids. Hell, she wasn't quite like most adults. And she'd never found someone who just loved her for who she was, who wanted her just the way she was without any strings attached.

Until now. And the knowledge set her whole world straight again. She could do anything with this man by her side. She could be anything she wanted to be, as long as she knew he would be there for her at the end of the day.

He reached up and stroked a tear from her eye. A tear, she hadn't realized had fallen, and she saw in his face that he was waiting as though she might say no, or tell him she didn't feel the same way.

She opened her mouth then, because she couldn't stand the thought that he might not know she loved him back. "I love you, too. So much. When I thought I might lose you . . .." She didn't finish because the thought of losing him had paralyzed her again.

He tugged her to him and she let him pull her in, right where she wanted to be. She didn't want to have to let him go into surgery.

"You won't lose me. I'm sticking around. I can't promise you this will be easy or that I won't need a ton of therapy for years to come, but I promise I'll keep working on it. I want you to know, I won't let my anger hurt you the way my dad hurt me and Laura with his anger. If I get to the point where things get bad and I'm taking it out on you, I'll take myself away while I work on my shit. But I'll always come back to you."

"I think we should try to do it together. You're in therapy, and really, you've only had one time where your anger took over. I understand you're afraid you'll be like your dad and hurt me, but why don't we agree that if we need to, we'll go see Sarah together and talk to her about ways to work on the anger."

He pulled her closer still and kissed her, threading his hand into her hair before breaking off the kiss to look at her. "I don't deserve you."

She smiled. "Of course you do. You deserve the world." She stopped when she realized what she'd said and shook her head, a grin breaking out on her face.

James laughed. "I think you just compared yourself to the world. I happen to agree, but still."

She pushed at his good shoulder as a nurse came into the room and started in on taking vitals and preparing him for the surgery that was to come. She'd waited so long for him. She'd almost lost him. Watching them wheel him out of the room half an hour later was one of the hardest things Presley had ever had to do.

She didn't have to wait alone. She had Hunt, the General, Laura, and Cade there with her, but her parents arrived shortly after James was taken in. She'd called them to let them know what had happened, but she was surprised to see they'd gotten to her so quickly.

Presley began to cry all over again when her mother and father wrapped their arms around her.

They both looked different somehow, but maybe it was just that they looked as exhausted as she felt. The last she knew, her mother had still been in their New York apartment.

Now, her mom felt up and down Presley's arms like she might find some injury the doctors had missed or some hurt Presley had hidden from them. "You're sure you're okay? I can't believe this happened."

Her mom's words broke off as tears streamed down her face and her father put his arms around her mom from behind. "She's all right, Kat."

It took her mind off of the surgery as she filled them in on what had happened. Her mom was pale as a ghost, shaking her head at Presley through most of it.

Then, they'd done the only thing they could do. They waited for news.

EPILOGUE

Presley looked around the room. The display shelves were perfect. James had also made coordinating free-standing shelving units that were spread around the center of Petals and Posies, each with the distinctive natural touches that made it evident each piece was an original work.

She had put off the grand opening of her store for a month. The shelves were filled with a variety of small plants, bonsai trees, and dried flower arrangements. Her refrigerated cases held more arrangements—these with fresh flowers. There were also cut flowers in lavender colored buckets in the refrigerators that would allow her to pull from them as clients told her what they wanted in a bouquet.

Outside, window boxes overflowed with colorful sprays and bunches, the warm Texas weather ensuring that she could keep them filled and blooming nearly year-round.

Presley took a deep breath and walked through to the work room in the back. The first few times she'd been back there, she'd had to have James with her to keep the panic of memories of being grabbed by her kidnappers at bay. In the past few weeks, they'd worked to replace the memories with happy ones of their own. Some of the memories were X-rated. Others were as simple as him helping to set up the space for her, replacing the plain work table with the custom-made table he'd finished for her.

He had needed Cade's help on the table since his arm was still in a sling for most of that time, but together, they'd gotten it done.

Now, James was setting the box of cinnamon rolls he'd just picked up from the diner onto the table and turning his smile her way. Lulu stood by his side, as always, but he was so different from the man who had barely said a word to her the day they first met.

"What are you smiling at?" He asked as he came her way, reaching out with his good arm to pull her in and kiss her. He didn't need his sling anymore, but he was still building the strength back in his left arm.

His kisses always rocked her a little. He had the power to set her head spinning so easily, it seemed.

"I'm just really happy," she said when he'd pulled back to look at her. "You make me so happy."

"It's mutual," he said, then looked around at the room they stood in. "You did it, Pres. You have your flower shop."

"You were a big part of it." They were waiting for her friends to arrive for a casual breakfast celebration before her official grand opening.

He made a face and shook his head, but she pressed the point.

"It's true. My mom's actions might have spurred me into action, but talking about it with you before that, having you there to cheer me on when I took the plunge, all of that meant something." She turned to the work table he'd made for her. "And this, all of the things you made for me that make the space so unique, they mean the world to me."

His eyes flashed with pleasure at her words and she realized she'd been seeing so much more of that in him lately. He was still seeing his therapist, and he was going to physical therapy to help his arm heal twice a week, but he was more relaxed now.

"I heard from Hunt this morning," he said, shifting the conversation.

"Yeah? How is he?"

"You'll find out soon. He called to let me know he'd packed up his truck and is heading our way. With Lars gone, he decided he didn't want to stay in Pennsylvania. He doesn't have family in the area or anything to tie him there, and he said he's a little burnt out with his work. He's going to head this way and stay for a while."

She smiled. "That's great. I love hanging out with Hunt."

He growled at her, but it was playful. He knew damned well she didn't have eyes for anyone but him. But, she meant what she said. She did like spending time with Hunt, mostly because James could laugh and have fun with him. James and Cade were growing closer, but James needed a friend in the area that understood him and what he'd been through.

There was a knock on the back door and James turned to pull it open.

The faces of all the people Presley loved came through the door. Laura, Cade and Jamie. Jamie squealed and reached for James, who took her with his good arm. Cade's brother, Shane, and his girlfriend, Phoebe, came next. Phoebe was General Brophy's daughter and she'd been the first one to track the fact that James was still alive and being held in South America. Without Phoebe and Shane, Presley wouldn't have James in her life. In fact, without them, he might be dead.

Laura was watching Jamie as she clung to James's neck. "Watch Uncle James's bad arm, Jamie," she warned.

The pair turned exasperated looks on her, answering, "He's fine" and "I'm fine," at the same time.

Cora and Emma entered next, followed by Ashley and Haddie. Garrett followed behind them with a carafe of hot coffee and a bag around his wrist. Haddie and Ashley set about stealing the bag from him and emptying its contents onto the table. They'd brought all the fixings for the coffee as well as cups and napkins.

Lily and her boyfriend, Carter, came in next followed by Katelyn and Sheriff John Davies, her husband. Katelyn had surprised them all the week before by announcing she was twelve weeks pregnant. She all but glowed now, but she said she'd been home throwing up for the past month.

Bringing up the rear were Presley's parents. After hugging everyone as they walked in, Presley went to her parents and hugged them. Her mom was living back at the Texas house now, but Presley got the sense things were still strained between them.

Her relationship with them was better than ever, though. Since the kidnapping, they'd been remarkably supportive of her decision to retire and open the shop. It seemed that a life-threatening situation could put things in perspective like nothing else.

Neither Presley nor James was the type for big toasts or anything like that, so the brunch was nothing more than what they enjoyed. A quiet visit with their closest friends. Food and coffee. And when the clock struck nine in the morning, they all walked to the front of the shop with

Presley as she turned the lock and flipped her *closed* sign to the *open* side.

Petals and Posies was open for business. No matter how the shop did, Presley could officially say she was never happier. Her life was hers, and it was whole.

DID you just love James's and Presley's story? I hope so! It was such a labor of love for me to write those two.

Next up is Treasure and Protect. I know you guys have wanted Cora and Justin to get their HEA for a long time! It's finally here! Grab Treasure and Protect now. loriryanromance.com/book/Treasure-and-Protect

Read on for chapter one of Treasure and Protect:

CHAPTER ONE

CORA WALKER WASN'T a stupid woman, but it was beginning to dawn on her that she *was* foolish at times.

Now was one of those times.

She had just caught herself fantasizing about Justin Kensington. Again.

She wondered if she'd ever get past her inane obsession with the blond-haired god. Sure, he had the kind of body that made you want to lick him like a lolly-pop, and yes, his eyes were mesmerizing in the extreme, but still. She should have more control than this, shouldn't she?

When he walked into the diner while she was waiting for her friend Laura Kensington to arrive, she'd caught herself imagining he might walk up to her. Instead of seeing the reality—which had been him saying hello to Presley and James across the room—she'd pictured him ignoring all the greetings from friends as he walked through the room to get to her. That kind of intense, single-minded focus you saw on a man's face in a movie when he saw the woman he wanted across a crowded room.

When he reached her, he'd put out his hand and draw her up from the table, then step into her space, standing just inside the line that said they were more than friends. He'd put one arm around her waist, letting his hand slide along her hip and around to her back. He'd press her to him, blue eyes sparkling with heat, and bend to whisper a personal hello in her ear.

She often had fantasies like this about Justin, despite the fact that he'd shown her time and again he had no interest in her other than as a friend.

Her sister was the romance novelist in the family. Somehow, Ashley always came up with these steamy, suspenseful plots filled with twists and turns that boggled Cora's mind. If Cora was writing a romantic suspense, she'd have lame little narrations, like: *in a stupidly handy turn of events, the heroine stumbled on a loaded weapon and turned to fire at her pursuer. She was a miraculously good shot for someone with no experience with a gun.*

Yeah, Cora wasn't an author for a reason. But with her fantasies about Justin, Cora could have given Ashley a run for her money.

They'd be at a party and she'd invent scenes where Justin drew her into a closet and stripped her bare, whispering for her to be quiet as he ravished her. In another, he'd dropped his beer bottle and lifted her so he could set her on a nearby table to kiss her properly.

"Properly" being with her legs and arms wrapped around him as he ground between her thighs.

She was welcomed back to the real world when Justin slid into the seat across from her.

"Hey, Cora. Meeting someone?" His dimples got her every time. He was like Robert Redford back in the '70s when he was super hot, only modern, not wearing shirts with big collars unbuttoned halfway to his knees.

Not that she'd mind his shirt unbuttoned halfway to his knees.

She mentally slapped herself. "Laura. We're having lunch."

Our heroine has resorted to stating the painfully obvious in an attempt at witty repartee with the hero.

He grinned at her.

"We have lunch sometimes," she mumbled. Lord, she couldn't stop herself.

Gina, one of the two sisters who owned and ran Two Sisters diner came to the table giving Cora the reprieve she badly needed.

"Still waitin' on one more?" she asked. Cora had already told her she was waiting for Laura.

"I can't stay. Tina's making me a sandwich to go," Justin said, with a nod of his head toward Tina, the other sister, who could be seen through the pass-through window that led to the kitchen.

It wasn't a surprise. When Justin first came to town, people hardly saw him. He stayed holed up in his house or office all the time. If you did see him, he wore a scowl that warned people away. Nowadays, he smiled more and he had friends, but he still worked much of the time. There was also a bit of the scowl left in him. It wasn't always on his face, but it was there. It was almost like he carried a heaviness with him wherever he went.

"That's a pretty necklace, Gina," Cora said. She leaned in. The necklace was heart shaped with small gems of various colors studding the heart.

Gina blushed, a hand going to the jewelry on her neck. "Thank you. The General got it for me."

No one had to ask who the General was. General Brophy came to town frequently nowadays, both to visit his daughter, Phoebe Joy, who was dating Shane Bishop, and to see his favorite waitress, Gina.

When Gina had moved on to a table across the room, Justin leaned in. "Do you think she calls him General in—"

Cora slapped her hands over her ears. "Don't say it. You're horrible!"

"What's horrible?" Laura asked, plopping herself on the seat next to Cora.

Justin was laughing as he got up and walked away.

Laura looked to Cora. "What did I miss?"

"You don't want to know." She searched for another topic. "Did you hear that Ron Knight filed his lawsuit?" The whole town had known the suit was coming.

"I did." Laura switched her seat to sit across from Cora now that Justin was gone. "I heard everyone talking about it the minute I walked through the door."

Two Sisters Diner was not only in the center of town physically, it was the center of town gossip. Cora didn't doubt that everyone there was talking about Mr. Knight and his lawsuit.

She sighed. "I'll find out how he's doing later today." She'd started visiting him on Sundays when he'd been diagnosed with a rare type of cancer. She hadn't stopped when he started telling everyone that Caufield Furniture had made him sick by mishandling the chemicals they used at an old storage facility near his land.

Sadly, his suit against the company was upsetting a lot of people. The company was one of the major employers in the area. People had depended on it for their livelihoods for decades. Seeing it threatened wasn't going over all that well, even if people felt for Mr. Knight and his neighbors, who'd all been diagnosed with significant illnesses.

Cora watched Justin pay for his sandwich and walk out. She knew he would be going back to the offices of the nonprofit he ran with Laura. He worked most weekends.

"Can I ask you something?" Cora asked, refocusing on Laura.

"Always."

"Do you think a person can just decide to get over someone they've been hung up on for a long time?"

Laura didn't try to pretend she didn't know who they were talking about. "I'd like to think he's going to wake up one of these days and see what he's missing. I happen to think you guys would be great together."

Laura was more than a friend of Justin's. Justin was her former husband's brother and they worked closely together running the nonprofit they'd started. If anyone knew Justin, it was Laura.

"I sense a but coming," Cora said.

"But," Laura said, with emphasis, "Justin has some issues and I don't know when he's going to get past those."

"Yeah," Cora said. She slumped down in her seat, sipping her club soda.

Laura tilted her head. "Can I ask you something now?"

"Always," Cora said, mimicking her friend's earlier response.

"Do you think you've been waiting all this time for him

to notice you because you want him, or do you think maybe you're focused on him because he's unattainable and you know it?"

Laura's words were soft but they cut just as if she'd put venom behind them.

Cora's denial was immediate. "Of course not."

Laura waited.

Cora laughed at her. "Really, it's not. I mean, that makes no sense."

There was no denying Laura was perceptive. She'd been taught to read other's emotions at a high cost during her previous marriage. Still, she was wrong here.

They were interrupted briefly when Gina came to take their orders, but Laura didn't let the subject drop. "Just think about it. It's just that, sometimes, people who have lost people early on in their lives do things to make sure they don't have to go through that again."

Cora was silent but she would be lying if she said Laura's suggestion didn't stick with her through the rest of the meal.

Even though her gut response had been that Laura was wrong, some part of her wondered if her friend might be right. Maybe it was time for a little more soul searching instead of just pouting over the fact her crush clearly saw her as nothing more than a friend. A completely platonic, asexual friend.

GET   TREASURE   AND   PROTECT   NOW!
loriryanromance.com/book/Treasure-and-Protect

I CAN NEVER THANK the people who help me with these books enough. This book wouldn't have been possible without the expertise of Karen Henderson, Bev Pettersen, Lynn Gaeckle-Avallone, Sarah Bond, and Dr. Ashley Hampton. Your quick assistance and expertise is so appreciated!

Clark Chamberlain, you helped this story come to life. Thank you so much for working with me to make this plot work.

I'd like to thank my amazing team of editors and beta readers. I couldn't do this without you guys.

As always, any errors are entirely mine.

ABOUT THE AUTHOR

Lori Ryan is a NY Times and USA Today bestselling author who writes romantic suspense, contemporary romance, and sports romance. She lives with an extremely understanding husband, three wonderful children, and two mostly-behaved dogs in Austin, Texas. It's a bit of a zoo, but she wouldn't change a thing.

Lori published her first novel in April of 2013 and hasn't looked back since then. She loves to connect with her readers.

For new release info and bonus content, join her newslettter here: loriryanromance.com/lets-keep-touch.

Follow her online:

facebook.com/loriryanromance

twitter.com/Loriryanauthor

instagram.com/loriryanauthor